Light Sleeper

Paul Schrader is a noted critic, screenwriter, and director. By his mid-twenties he had already been a film reviewer for the *L.A. Free Press*, while a graduate student at UCLA; editor of his own magazine, *Cinema;* Fellow in Criticism of the American Film Institute; and author of the uncompromising *Transcendental Style in Film: Ozu, Bresson, Dreyer.* By the mid-seventies he was one of Hollywood's most successful screenwriters, eventually writing three films for Martin Scorsese: *Taxi Driver, Raging Bull,* and *The Last Temptation of Christ.* His directorial achievements include *Blue Collar, American Gigolo, Cat People, Mishima,* and *The Comfort of Strangers.*

also published by Faber

SCHRADER ON SCHRADER
TAXI DRIVER

Light Sleeper

Paul Schrader

faber and faber

LONDON · BOSTON

Introduction © Kevin Jackson and Paul Schrader, 1992
Photo of Paul Schrader © Chris Callas
Stills © Grain of Sand Productions 1991

CIP records for this book are available from the British Library and the Library of Congress

Printed in the United States of America

ISBN 0-571-16649-0

Contents

Paul Schrader

Introduction

KEVIN JACKSON: There are some obvious echoes of *Taxi Driver* in the script for *Light Sleeper*. Were the similarities between the two films planned from the outset, or did they arise from the nature of the subject matter?

PAUL SCHRADER: Well, the format of the script is the same as the format of *Taxi Driver*, in that it uses pseudo-chapters rather than scene numbers, but the deeper connection comes from the fact that this is a character that I have felt comfortable with in the past and hadn't written about in some time. As to the specific moments – well, you don't want to be too self-referential, but if it works, it works, and if you're ploughing the same row ten or fifteen years on, you're going to end up with the same roots being dug up. The character of John LeTour is, in my mind, another installment of the characters of Travis Bickle in *Taxi Driver* and Julian Kay in *American Gigolo*. These characters are really not so much people as souls, they drift around and things happen to them, they watch and they are acted upon. I don't really see this group of films as a trilogy, I just think that as I get older my views about this character and these themes change. So that when the character and myself were in our twenties, he was very hostile and paranoid and felt oppressed by the world, and was a cab driver. When he was in his thirties he was very narcissistic and self-involved, and he was a gigolo. Now he's forty and he's anxious and uncertain, and he delivers drugs. He hasn't made anything of his life, and he doesn't know what will become of him.

JACKSON: So in that sense *Light Sleeper* is a film about a mid-life crisis?

SCHRADER: Yes, in the very direct sense that it's about a man who doesn't know what to do next – his boss is about to leave and go into the cosmetics business and he has no marketable skills. He's been a dealer for ten, twelve years. Also, as a result of this situation he starts to worry: he consults a psychic and his worries grow to the point where they become distorted, and he starts to see events somewhat inaccurately; he starts to see a conspiracy. But I think that what we call a mid-life crisis is really just a life crisis, it's that period in your life when you realize that you are what you are going to be. All these characters I've written about are looking for a place to fit, but as they get older, the eagerness or the anger to make a place for themselves subsides.

JACKSON: What were the circumstances of writing the script?

SCHRADER: Well, another connection with *Taxi Driver* is the speed with which I wrote *Light Sleeper*. *Taxi Driver* was written nonstop, but I'm older now and have to keep family hours, so I couldn't write around the clock, but it was the same type of energy, and I finished the script in two weeks. It came to me pretty much as a piece; I saw it all, and I always knew what was going to come next. What happened was that I had a dream about this character sometime in September 1990, somebody I had known years before. I woke up at about four in the morning, and I knew from that moment that he wanted me to write about him. By six I also knew I was definitely going to do just that. I hadn't written about this type of character in almost ten years. I'd been looking around for a personal, original piece to write and it hadn't been coming, so I had given up, and then it just came. So I set off to track down this man I had known.

JACKSON: And did you find him?

SCHRADER: Yes, and he helped me with research, but for reasons of discretion and professional courtesy I can't say much more than that.

JACKSON: Portraying drugs and drug dealers without taking up an overtly censorious attitude is not likely to win a writer many fans these days. Did that worry you?

SCHRADER: Just the opposite: that's what got me going. The idea of taking a would-be presidential assassin and making him a hero, or making a male prostitute a hero – that's absolutely invigorating, because it's the element of originality that can run against the grain and create sparks, give a character depth. It's tricky, too, because you have to make this character sympathetic without making him ersatz. I think that's quite possible, because these people who do these day-to-day evil and demeaning things are not actually evil themselves, and it's easy to identify with their daily routines.

JACKSON: Was one of the impulses behind *Light Sleeper* a documentary ambition, the wish to show exactly what those routines are?

SCHRADER: Yes, because these are interesting characters who haven't been in the movies before. When people think of drug dealers they have very broad stereotypical images — sort of Hispanics with Uzis — and this is a peculiar, middle-class family grouping.

JACKSON: Yes, the relationship between Ann, John, and Robert reads almost like a parody of life in a rather conventional, but mother-dominated, family. Was this invention, or something you had observed among dealers?

SCHRADER: It was something I saw. Big Momma and her boys.

JACKSON: Are there any points of similarity between the three different occupations of this protagonist of yours across the three films?

SCHRADER: They're all sort of non-people. They appear in other people's lives to perform a service, and they're all terribly important to their clients when their clients don't have them, but the second they've done their job they become non-people; they vanish before your eyes. And therefore they see life from the outside, they drift about, watch the high and the low, the educated and the vulgar, and they're sort of detached from it all. Really quite pure at an intellectual level. It's like the character in *Taxi Driver* says, "I'll take anybody, it doesn't matter to me." It's that kind of cold detachment that allows them to be part of the world but not really in it, and to be incorporeal in a way, like souls that are looking for a body to inhabit.

JACKSON: One of the chapter headings in *Light Sleeper* is

Confessor LeTour," and there is a sense in which all these three characters are like confessors or analysts—they're available for hire to people who need to talk, like the jealous husband played by Scorsese in *Taxi Driver*.

SCHRADER: Though there's no communication. These are people who are in communication with themselves, but not with others.

JACKSON: Why the more abstract title *Light Sleeper* rather than, say, *Dealer* or *Connection* or some other vocational label?

SCHRADER: I would have preferred to have a vocational title, but there really was none that didn't stereotype the film in such a way that you couldn't ever get across the type of film you were dealing with. *Dealer* wasn't good, *Delivery Boy* wasn't good, *Drug Dealer* wasn't good. Drug dealers sometimes call themselves "D.D.s" or "D.D.ers," but *D.D.er* isn't a good title either. So I took the title from the fact that this character has reached the point in his life where he can't really get through a night, and then there was a text from Corinthians that I remembered and that made an ideal epigraph.

JACKSON: As soon as you'd written the script, you took it immediately to Willem Dafoe. Why was he your first choice?

SCHRADER: I was so hot on the idea that I didn't even pitch it to anyone to get money. My agent even tried to dissuade me from writing it, because he felt it was an uncommercial subject, but I had very strong feelings about it. So now I had a script that I owned and could make right away, and it was a question of who was available. I had met Willem during *Last Temptation*, and was so impressed by what he did on the film, and I also thought he looked very much like my idea of LeTour—there's a certain pallor, a certain quality these dealers have. So I had dinner with Willem, found out that he was available, and he agreed to do the film the next day.

JACKSON: Did Dafoe's commitment make the film easier to finance?

SCHRADER: No; and then I was told that it would make it easier to finance if I got someone of Susan Sarandon's caliber, so I set forth and got Susan Sarandon, and it *still* wasn't easy to finance. Eventually I did manage it, albeit with financial sacrifices by everyone involved in the production: Willem and Susan worked for a fraction of their usual salaries, I deferred my fees, and I cash-flowed preproduction out of my own pocket. But I don't consider my own sacrifices earth-shaking. Just because people get paid so much in movies, it doesn't mean that it's a greater sacrifice when they do what most artists do, which is finance their own art. Most novelists don't get paid more than a pittance until their books are published, and the same applies to a lot of painters and composers, but when a screenwriter says, "I'll forego my fee," he's treated like some kind of saint.

JACKSON: But why were you so eager to get this particular film made?

SCHRADER: I felt I knew it, it already existed in my head: the embryo was growing, and it got better the more I dealt with it and thought about it. And I guess it was a test to

myself in a way, to see whether I could still work this territory.

JACKSON: In the draft which was meant to be definitive at the time shooting began, a great deal of the script was taken up with quotations from two Bob Dylan albums, *Empire Burlesque* and *Oh Mercy*, which were going to provide the film's musical setting. What was the intention of that, and why have those songs now gone?

SCHRADER: I wanted the film to have a ballad structure, with a chorus that kept coming in, so that there was a third voice for the main character. You had his dialogue voice, and then you had his diary voice, and then you had the balladeer's voice, which would throw a third perspective on this closed-off man. I liked a lot of the Dylan songs and thought that they were very apropos, with their apocalyptic, Biblical imagery and all that rabbinical soulfulness, so I put them in the script. It turned out that Bob did not want to cooperate fully – he would give certain songs under certain conditions, but not all the songs I wanted, and he was just difficult. So I've now gone to a singer-songwriter named Michael Been, from a group called the Call, and they are taking a similar approach: six original songs, plus scoring, plus singing. Incidentally, Michael had a part in *The Last Temptation of Christ*, where he played the apostle John.

JACKSON: It seems unusual to have music and lyrics quite so strongly and frequently signaled in a script.

SCHRADER: It hasn't been done much. Lindsay Anderson tried it in *O Lucky Man!*, though I don't know whether those lyrics were ever in the script, and there he put the singer, Alan Price, on-screen, which was not something I wanted to do. *Pat Garrett and Billy the Kid* has this same quality, and I'm sure film buffs can point out other films in which a single voice has performed songs as a narrative thread. I wanted to have something musical which would underline the moments when the hero goes back to the road, back to the road, always cut to the road. In *Taxi Driver* it was the Tom Scott sax solo that brought you back, in *American Gigolo* it was the Giorgio Moroder music that brought you back, and here it will be the chorus or verse of a ballad.

JACKSON: One of the most noticeable things about the script is its habit of referring to or hinting at occult matters—psychics, numerology, Madame Blavatsky. Is this just atmospheric, a factual detail about the superstitions of drug dealers, or is it also thematic in some way?

SCHRADER: Well, it originated in dealing with these people at a research level, and finding that all of them were involved in paranormal pursuits to some degree. Even if they didn't have psychic sessions or sign readings, card readings, palm readings, they were all very interested in the phenomenon of extra-physical powers. And I think it's because they all believe in this particular theory of luck. They think that they are able to read situations, to read the aura of a meeting and therefore know when to walk away and not get busted. They think it's a psychic power, psychic luck, that has kept them going. The idea of being "in the groove of a situation," as they put it, very quickly moves over to the question of whether you're in tune with your own self and with the psychic forces around you. It struck me that this whole notion of luck is very similar to the Christian notion of Providence, and that appealed to me very much.

JACKSON: Your cinematographer on *Light Sleeper,* Ed Lachman, says that one of the things you did before the shoot began was to look at some early films by Antonioni. You've mentioned in the past that this is a common practice of yours, but that the kind of ideas you might take from these viewings don't necessarily end up on the screen. What has happened this time?

SCHRADER: Antonioni is always good to look at because he loves to define situations by architecture. When you're getting ready to direct, you're just at the point where you're trying to think: "What is the visual equivalent of this scene? What situation can I put these people in, how can I photograph them, so that what they are saying is redundant and I can actually cut out lines because I can *see* what they're saying?" So you turn to the filmmakers who are good on composition and architectural sentiment— because that's the point that you are at in the evolution of the idea. I mean, you wouldn't watch an Antonioni film *before* you sat down to write a script.

JACKSON: So a lot of this is to do with placing the character in an environment, and understanding him because of where he is and how he stands?

SCHRADER: Yes, and having enough courage to make some bold statements visually. There isn't any direct reference to Antonioni in the finished film.

JACKSON: In *Taxi Driver* you wrote one of the definitive films about New York, but this is the first film you've ever shot here. Was it just chance that you've avoided the city before, and was there any special reason for working here now?

SCHRADER: *Taxi Driver* had to be set in New York, because it's the only American city where road transportation is really ruled by taxis, and it seemed natural to set *Gigolo* in L.A. because L.A. is that kind of moral world. "Dial-a-Drug," which is what this delivery service is called, is more New York. You can find it in any major city around the world, but in New York it's big and sophisticated because the market is big and sophisticated. In another city he might do his own driving, but in New York you need a driver because you can't park, and you have to pay someone to wait while you deliver. So you're in a very passive environment. In many ways, the difference between *Taxi Driver* and *Light Sleeper* is that in the first film the protagonist is in the front seat and in this film he's in the back seat.

JACKSON: And the running joke about LeTour, Ann, and Robert always ordering take-away food is a commentary on the kind of business they're engaged in themselves? They have to dial out for their needs, too.

SCHRADER: They have to stay close to the phone.

JACKSON: The time of *Light Sleeper* is a Labor Day weekend, in the middle of a sanitation strike. Why that date and that background?

SCHRADER: No great significance; there's always a strike of some sort going on in the city, and some of them are more obvious and smelly and inconveniencing than others. Certainly a subway strike wouldn't be particularly inconveniencing for this man, but a sanitation strike is something he has to deal with because he's on the streets all the time.

JACKSON: How did you arrive at the name "LeTour," which is fairly exotic?

SCHRADER: I liked the idea of "touring," because he's on a tour and it's a tourist kind of part, and "Tour," or *tueur* is a French word meaning "killer." To make that pun work you needed a French prefix on it.

JACKSON: Why did you decide to use the convention of chapter headings you've mentioned?

SCHRADER: When you write a script you're writing it for a reader, not a viewer, and that's always a difference of approach. What you're trying to create in the reader's mind is this episodic world—another episode, another event, this happens, this happens, and then this happens . . . and there's a kind of hypnotic rhythm to it. And I find that giving scene numbers and a direct linear page count is not as hypnotic as giving chapter headings and white spaces.

JACKSON: Was there something appealing about returning, after working on other kinds of scripts, to the type of structure in which your hero is in every single scene?

SCHRADER: He's not only *in* every scene, a scene doesn't begin until he's in it and it doesn't last after he leaves it. You are not privy to the world about him. I like that sort of visual monopoly; it's like seeing life through a long tube, and you know that a thousand things are happening around but you can only see through the end of the tube. Everything is built on accretion of detail. The main character is passive; he lets the movie roll over him like waves on the beach. The waves will always come, but he will always be there. One of the things that Willem and I worked on was that he should never try to take a scene, never try to dominate it. Essentially, I said to him, "You're always going to be there on-screen, these other people are going to come and go, so just give the scenes away one after another, because in the end your character will emerge from this passivity, it doesn't need to be *stated*."

JACKSON: You're almost finished with editing now. Did you have to lose anything from the shooting script?

SCHRADER: At the moment, I'm dropping the scene where he visits Robert toward the end, because it seems wrong for the pace of the movie at that point. But it's a nice scene, and I kind of like it because it puts the theme of the movie into the mouth of the Fool, the blatherer. It's sort of a Shakespearean trick: Robert talks about "there's a plan unfolding, you've gotta get with the plan, don't fight the flow," all this kind of stuff, which is basically what the movie's about, but he's saying it in such a jerky way that he sounds like an asshole.

JACKSON: You make it sound a little like Wizard's speech from *Taxi Driver*, when he gives his "philosophical" advice to Travis Bickle.

SCHRADER: Right, it's the same thing, so maybe it's good that I've cut it because it's probably a little too close to that scene, a little too close to *Taxi Driver*.

JACKSON: There seems to be a note of redemption at the end of the film.

SCHRADER: I'm not so sure I'd call it redemption; it's certainly a sense of "the wind bloweth where it will."

JACKSON: Do you think that you'll be going back to this type of solitary, drifting character again in later films?

SCHRADER: You never know. If he remains fresh, and if the audience still thinks he's fresh this time around, then there's always that possibility of seeing what's become of him ten years further down. If it's clear to me after this film that he's not a character that strikes the popular imagination, then maybe I won't pick up on him again. But I do think that he's still a valid character.

New York
Labor Day weekend, 1991

Light Sleeper was released in 1992. The cast includes:

LETOUR	Willem Dafoe
ANN	Susan Sarandon
MARIANNE	Dana Delany
ROBERT	David Clennon
TERESA	Mary Beth Hurt
TIS	Victor Garber
RANDI	Jane Adams

Casting	Ellen Chenoweth
Editor	Kristina Boden
Music	Michael Been
Production Designer	Richard Hornung
Director of Photography	Ed Lachman
Co-Executive Producer	Ronna B. Wallace
Co-Producer	G. Mac Brown
Executive Producer	Mario Kassar
Producer	Linda Reisman
Written and Directed by	Paul Schrader

Stills by Steve Sands and Demmie Todd
A Grain of Sand Production

"Behold I show you a mystery; we shall not all sleep, but we shall all be changed."

I. Corinthians 15:51

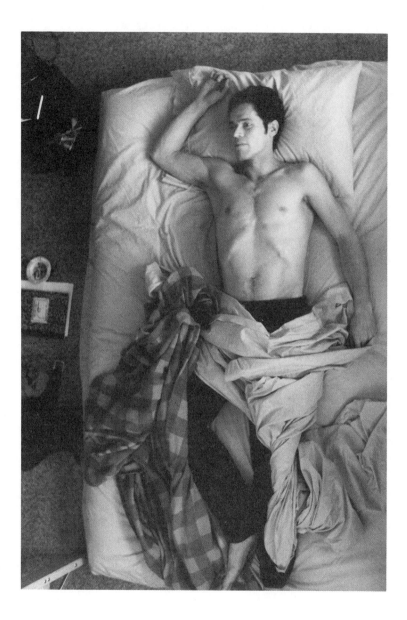

JOHN LETOUR, *forty, light sleeper. Never meant to be a drug dealer, it just came along. He's been other things: messenger boy, cab driver, model, postal clerk, doorman, nightclub shill—never meant to be them either. Now he's a D.D. Drug dealer.*

JOHN LETOUR, *well-groomed, khaki slacks, leather jacket, tippet-like scarf, belt pouch, "Beatle" boots, a shadow drifting in and out of other shadows, New York, day, night: watching, listening, rarely speaking—nonexistent, seen only by those he sees. His face an affable blank. Make of it what you will. The eyes flicker; the hands shift discreetly. A map of calculation.*

Once he had a drug problem. Life turned a page. Today he follows instructions: he sleeps light—one eye open, anticipating.

JOHN LETOUR, *D.D., loner, voyeur, has been drifting toward an unknown destination. At mid-life the destination draws near. The circle tightens. The dealer is anxious. The destination is love.*

A NIGHT IN THE LIFE

CREDIT SEQUENCE: *New York by night.* JOHN LETOUR *nestles in back of a blue car service sedan, face reflected in the window. Neon mixes with steam, street people with tourists, young dates: each with a different agenda, a hidden purpose.*

His beeper goes off. He clicks it, checks the digital message. The DRIVER *stops at an uptown corner.* LETOUR *opens the curbside door, motions to the* DRIVER *he'll be back in "ten" minutes. He enters the video laundromat, a twenty-four-hour video rental/laundromat/tanning salon.*

Inside, he meets a RETRO-YUPPIE (*J. Crew Division*) *in the "Classics" section. They exit.*

On the sidewalk, money is exchanged for a packet. LETOUR *pockets the uncounted cash. The* YUPPIE *mouths* goodbye, *eager to put distance between him and* LETOUR. JOHN *checks his beeper, stops at a pay phone, dials.*

JOHN LETOUR *re-enters the sedan; the* DRIVER *heads downtown. High-rises give way to Tudor City. Uncollected trash lines the curbs.* LETOUR *eyes a* PEDESTRIAN; PEDESTRIAN *looks back. Later. Three a.m. The streets are dark. LeTour's car passes a glowing Korean market.*

LETOUR *narrates from diary:*

LETOUR: (*Voice over*) Labor Day weekend. Some time for a
sanitation strike. Everybody crazy to stock up. They
decide to score at the last minute and want it now. Never
fails. The faces look alike. You gotta use memory tricks:
each has some peculiarity – it keeps you sharp. A D.D.
told me when a drug dealer starts writing a diary it's time
to quit. I started writing after that. Not every night – now
and then. Just to burn off the night. Fill up one book,
throw it out, start another.

(*The sedan drives on. End credits.*)

CUT TO:

HOMEBASE

*Four a.m.: streets empty. LeTour's sedan drops him off near a
ten-story West 80s apartment building.* JOHN *gives the* DRIVER *a
forty-dollar tip (standard procedure), turns the corner. He presses
the intercom; a buzzer unlocks the door. He enters the lobby,
walks past English reproduction furniture toward the elevators.
Presses the button.*

Penthouse C door opens. ANN *lets* JOHN *in with a smile.*

ANN, *forty-four, striking in a tailored dress, greets him with a wet
kiss. Her hair is coiffured, her face made up. She is John's
employer, mentor, confidante, Mother Hen: she keeps the books.
Her ingenuous demeanor belies sterner stuff: she's been in the drug
business fifteen years.*

*Ann's apartment is a jumble of sensibilities: dark green walls,
zebra-skin sofa, Haitian wall friezes, framed magazine photos of
Paramahansa Yogananda, Liz Taylor, the Duke of Windsor –
paintings stacked behind an oversized urn. A bird flits in its cage.
One corner of the living area is devoted to a fledgling cosmetics
business: Macintosh computer, billboard of trade paper clippings
and ads, herbal samples, reference books, color charts.*

ROBERT, *fifty, slight, waves hello as* JOHN *locks the door. Gay,
hip, worn, he's John's "co-runner."*

*They work – and eat – out of Ann's apartment. Take-out tins of
Indian food are stacked amid crystals, tarot cards, glasses, and
vitamin bottles. No sign of drugs, drug paraphernalia, or money.*

ANN: Darling.

LETOUR: Ann.

ANN: Have we made New York safe for another weekend?

LETOUR: (*Waves*) Robert.

ROBERT: Get a job.

LETOUR: (*About* ROBERT) Sad what ten years without sex can do.
(*Repartee: the plumbing of family feeling.*
JOHN *unzips his belt pouch, walks toward the bedroom to*
deposit the night's earnings.)

ANN: Any hundreds?

LETOUR: Twenties – and tens.

ROBERT: Tens!

ANN: Goddamn cash machines.

ROBERT: Did what's-his-name give you a hard time?

LETOUR: (*Out of shot*) You mean – ?

ROBERT: Yeah.

LETOUR: Cash Before Delivery. (*Re-emerges.*) CBD.

ROBERT: Fucking investment bankers.

ANN: These Wall Street kids deal with fake money all day,
they think cash is a theoretical concept – like it doesn't
apply. I see 'em at two, shudder to think at nine they're
buying and selling – turned me off the stock market.

4

LETOUR: It's late.
(*To* ROBERT.)
You staying?
ROBERT: It's over.
LETOUR: I'm gonna crash – try, at least.
ANN: (*To* LETOUR) Tomorrow will be easier. Maybe we can all
eat together. Go on. You look tired. Here, take a couple
of C's. I'll pick up anything that comes in.
(LETOUR *turns to leave.*)
ANN: Sleep tight.
ROBERT: Pick up the trash.
LETOUR: (*Laughs*) Yeah – big kiss.
(*He throws two kisses, exits.*)

CUT TO:

JOHN'S APARTMENT

First light reflects across the Hudson as LETOUR *walks west on
22nd Street toward his Chelsea apartment building. A delivery
truck passes uncollected garbage. He enters a nondescript doorway.
Inside his studio apartment,* JOHN *sits at a second-hand table
writing in a composition book. He drinks from an eight-ounce
glass of white wine, continues.*
*The room has little personality; Ann's apartment has enough for
two. Nails indicate where pictures once hung; a boombox sits on
the linoleum floor amid cassettes, books* (Autobiography of a
Yogi, The Secret Doctrine), *fashion magazines, a stack of
unopened CDs. A futon is unrolled beneath the room's sole
decoration, a poster of a human foot advertising a forgotten photo
exhibit. Wine bottles – Chenin Blanc. Precious little to show for
forty years.*
LeTour's narration resumes as he writes:
LETOUR: (*Voice over*) "Labor Day." "Union Movement" –
there's a contradiction in terms. I know about long hours.
It's worse when I'm off – I just walk and walk. Where am
I going? There's an element of providence to it all. Like
rolling numbers. Luck. You're walking down the street,
some guy that looks maybe a little like you does a stick-up
four hours ago, there's an APB description out and a cop

5

pulls you in cause he's cold and wants to go inside – they grab your stash. Your number's up. You're busted for nothing. For bad luck.

CUT TO:

JEALOUS

Five p.m. A Clinton transient hotel.
Inside hotel room, LETOUR *meets with* JEALOUS, *a twenty-five-year-old drug intermediary in leather jacket.* JOHN *counts hundred-dollar bills, hands them to* JEALOUS.
JEALOUS: Are they "faced"?
LETOUR: Don't bore me.
    (JEALOUS *rearranges the hundreds:*)
JEALOUS: Is it so much work to face them the same direction? You don't do it, I got to. It's time – my time –
LETOUR: (*Overlap*) Jees –
JEALOUS: We've been through all this.
    (LETOUR *shrugs.*)
    This nineteen-gram shit is a drag.
LETOUR: We pay you more, you put up with more. White drugs for white people. Twice the price, twice the safety.
JEALOUS: I can't believe Ann's been working as long as she has – never busted. She's something.
LETOUR: Never made any big money either.
JEALOUS: Sure.
LETOUR: She blows it.
JEALOUS: You believe that? What you gonna do after she quits? How long you been with her?
LETOUR: She always says that. We'll see, Jealous.
JEALOUS: She's out. You should pick up her trade. You're too old to be a go-fer. They know you, they trust you.
LETOUR: No way. I'm not the management type. I get in charge, I'll start using again – not for me. I know music people. I'm gonna get in recording.
JEALOUS: Yeah.
    (LETOUR *reaches for the door.*)
JEALOUS: Tour.
LETOUR: What?

6

JEALOUS: Normally this wouldn't matter to you, but you may get hassled.

LETOUR: Why?

JEALOUS: You read the papers? The Park murder. All over the *Post*. Mariah Rangel – nineteen-year-old Barnard co-ed bitch dead in Turtle Pond coked to the fucking gills. All of a sudden they're hot after mid-level dealers. They're buzzin'. You know her?

LETOUR: (*Shrugs*) I look like an encyclopedia? Who knows? (*Opens door.*)
Thanks for the warning.

CUT TO:

THE NIGHT BEGINS

Ann's apartment. Eight p.m. She opens the door for LETOUR, *kisses him, goes back to the phone. Mantra muzak plays as* JOHN *locks door, heads toward bedroom. Inside bedroom, MTV glows silently as* ROBERT, *wearing a black turtleneck, works at a desk amid tools of the trade: digital scale, "hot box," Deering grinder, block of manite, pure cocaine, pills, felt pen.* ROBERT *scissors glossy magazine paper* (Elle) *into neat quarters, folds each into gram-size "bindels"–envelopes. Red satin drapes the ceiling.*

ROBERT: Jack.

(JOHN *kisses him atop the head.*)

ROBERT: You pick up from Jealous?

LETOUR: (*Passes bag*) Yeah, nineteen grams after four times last night. We're certainly not his favorite people.

ROBERT: We don't make the laws. Nineteen is carrying, twenty is dealing. Let him be stupid.

LETOUR: He took my hundreds.

ROBERT: (*Stands*) Take over for a while. I'm getting contact high.

LETOUR: (*Sits*) Who's Her Majesty talking to?

(ROBERT *flips through cable channels as* JOHN *grinds cocaine.*)

ROBERT: The Ecstasy connection. From Arizona. She's trying to get them to come here – or, better, Europe.

LETOUR: That's where the money is.

7

ROBERT: All mark-up—the "Big One."

LETOUR: (*Laughs*) Don't dress. (*Beat.*) You really think she means it?

ROBERT: That's what she says. New Year's Eve and out—no Acid House, no product, no deliveries.

LETOUR: That's just her mouth talking.

ROBERT: Next year—strictly Akasha.

LETOUR: "Akasha"?

ROBERT: Cosmetics. That's what Ann's calling the company now—

LETOUR: (*Interjects*) —this week. I don't get it—marigolds, violets, sage—why'd anyone pay to put weeds on their face?

ROBERT: Why'd anyone pay to put them up their nose? I like cosmetics. I *need* cosmetics. You should come in with us.

LETOUR: You forget: she hasn't asked me.

(ANN *hangs up, calls:*)

ANN: (*Out of shot*) Johnny! Robert! Come here!

(*They return to the living area.*)

ANN: (*Open arms*) Plant me two kisses, boys, fifteen hundred Ex at thirty each and the delivery's here.

(*They simultaneously kiss her cheeks.*)

ANN: (*To* LETOUR) Whatja think?

LETOUR: Of what?

ANN: The face cream. Almond, marigold, chamomile, egg, aloe—the "Almilk" formula. I remixed it.

LETOUR: (*Smells her*) Very nice.

ANN: Reminds me, if you get downtown stop at Enhancements and pick up some almond oil—not the California. (*Fishes menus from desk.*) What should we order?

LETOUR: How about Indian?

ANN: Darling, it's Saturday.

ROBERT: Thai. We haven't had Thai in a while.

(*The phone rings. Ann's voice repeats a recorded message:*)

ANN'S VOICE: "Hello. This is Ann. If you leave a message, we'll get back to you—sooner than you think."

(*Answering machine beeps.* MAN'S VOICE *speaks from the tiny speaker:* "Ann, this is Ed. Call me. 749-2876.")

ANN: (*To* ROBERT) Answer that. He'll call back every five minutes.

8

ROBERT: (*Walking*) The night begins.

(*The phone rings again: another message as* ANN *examines the menu.*)

ANN: "Ped Srilom"?—it's Northeastern. Duck.

LETOUR: (*Glancing*) I'm going veggie. Get me the "Puk Ob."

ROBERT: (*Out of shot from phone*) Me too.

LETOUR: Use it for facial cream.

ROBERT: (*Out of shot*) Remove unsightly hair!

ANN: Laugh, one day you'll be watching me on "Oprah" from a welfare hotel.

LETOUR: Forgive us.

ROBERT: (*Returns*) Eddie wants now. Now. His place. Top Lady. God knows what happened to his shit yesterday.

ANN: (*To* LETOUR) You take it—call in.

LETOUR: It was supposed to be light tonight.

ROBERT: Don't you watch TV?

LETOUR: Don't have one.

ROBERT: Well if you were the normal stupid fuck you should

9

be so lucky to be and had one, you'd know it's supposed
to rain—

ANN: Good for the trees—

ROBERT: Some farmer whacked his numerology on us.

ANN: (*Peers through curtain*) It's started.

ROBERT: The Farmer's Almanac is based on numerology.

LETOUR: Raining?

ANN: Take a coat.

(*To* ROBERT.)

And you, clean up the product before the food delivery
comes.

(JOHN *grabs his belt pouch, heads for the closet.*)

CUT TO:

CONFESSOR LETOUR

*Rain falls on LeTour's car near an East Side luxury high-rise.
The door opens to Eddie's apartment: severe decor, once chic, now
dated.* EDDIE, *thirty-two, is a mess: puffy face, sweaty shirt,
pinched lips—on a drug jag.*

EDDIE: LeTour!—finally. What took so long?

LETOUR: (*Steps inside*) Traffic. It's raining.

EDDIE: How's things?

LETOUR: Okay.

EDDIE: I need a quarter—you got it?

LETOUR: (*Nods*) Robert said he sold you a quarter yesterday.

EDDIE: (*Slurs*) Some friends came over. How much is that?
Fourteen-hundred?

(LETOUR *nods as* EDDIE, *employing diminished skills, counts
from a roll of twenties.* JOHN *looks around: full ashtrays,
porn tapes, empty vodka bottles—there have been no
"friends."*)

LETOUR: Eddie. Look at yourself. Sit down. I've known you,
what, like eight years?

EDDIE: (*Counting*) Yeah . . .

LETOUR: Knew you from the other job, the one before the last
one you fucked up. I knew your wife—remember her? We
used to sit and talk and talk— (*Pressures* EDDIE *into chair.*)

EDDIE: (*Whining*) You don't know what she was like—

10

LETOUR: This is no good. I'll sell you a gram and some downs, but I ain't gonna put you in the emergency room. Cool it. Go to bed. Sleep it off.
(*John's beeper goes off.*)
EDDIE: (*Stands*) You charge $200 for what goes for ninety on the street – and you're not gonna sell?
LETOUR: (*Clicks beeper*) So go to the street.
EDDIE: I'll call Ann.
LETOUR: Go ahead. You know what she'll say. Phone's over there.
EDDIE: (*Irrational*) I'll tell the fucking cops.
LETOUR: (*Flashes cold*) Fuck you. That's it. You're out. (*Turns to leave.*) Don't call again. Catch you next lifetime.
EDDIE: (*Contrite*) Please, Tour, I'm sorry. You're right. I didn't mean that. I'm quitting anyway. I'll take the gram. Sorry.
LETOUR: (*Turns back*) Okay.
EDDIE: Two hundred?

(LETOUR *nods.*

EDDIE *counts $200 as* LETOUR *takes a gram from his pouch, gives it to him.*)

LETOUR: You got downs?

(EDDIE *nods.*)

One more thing. I gotta use the phone.

(EDDIE *pockets the envelope as* JOHN, *checking his beeper, walks to the phone.*

Later. LETOUR *sits in an Upper West Side apartment as an earnest* MID-TWENTIESH MAN, *wearing undershorts, snorts a hefty line, offers a rolled dollar bill as he talks.* LETOUR *declines.*)

MID-TWENTIESH MAN: (*Continuing*) . . . but—if there's no God, how can man conceive of him? The idea of God presupposes the existence of God. That's the Ontological Argument. Anselm. Twelve hundred. Fourteen hundred—I'm not sure—

LETOUR: (*Checks his watch*) I've got to go.

MID-TWENTIESH MAN: (*Gesturing*) Let me finish. Okay, if the idea of God is implanted by God—the *sensus divinitatus*, the sense of the divine—what is the role of human thought? Not faith, thought . . .

(LETOUR's *mind drifts. His diary voice overlaps:*)

LETOUR: (*Voice over*) Everybody wants to talk. It's like a compulsion. My philosophy is: you got nothing to say, don't say it. They figure you can tell a D.D. anything, things they would never tell anyone else. He understands. Of course they're stoned to start. If I could tie together all the hours of coke talk I've heard, that would be a lot of string. It was Robert's idea to add twenty-five dollars to home deliveries cause it's such a hassle. Fifty is more like it.

(*Later. Narration continues as sedan drives through rain. Later. A Tribeca loft.* LETOUR *swaps drug jargon with* TWO N.Y.U. STUDENTS *at an impromptu party. Attractive ingenues drift by.* TRENDY TWOSOME, *blasted, sways to techno-rap.*

Business done, LETOUR *turns to leave. The* FIRST STUDENT *grabs his shoulder:*)

FIRST STUDENT: C'mon, Tour, stick around.

SECOND STUDENT: Yeah.

FIRST STUDENT: There's only four of us and like seven of them—and we're paying for the dope. See her, over there, the blonde, long hair, yellow skirt?—she's gonna model for Elite.

(DOWNTOWN NYMPH, *sixteen going on seventeen.*)

LETOUR: (*Smiling*) Me? I'm an old man. She'd break me like an old horse.

SECOND STUDENT: Shit, dude—

LETOUR: Nah. Thanks anyway. (*Checks watch.*) I gotta go. Have fun. (*Heads toward exit.*)

CUT TO:

A FACE FROM THE PAST

LeTour's sedan heads down Lexington Avenue. It rains unabated. Puddles glisten; red taillights refract on the windshield. JOHN *rests in back, a bag from Enhancements beside him.*

Pedestrians, well-dressed and casual, desperately wave for taxis amid sacks of garbage. No use: nothing for blocks.

John's sedan stops for a midtown light. LETOUR *looks out the window, sees a* WOMAN *vainly hailing a cab. He looks again. She turns her head. He recognizes her.*

LETOUR: (*To* DRIVER) Carlos. Wait a second.

(*He leans over, opens the far door, calls:*)

LETOUR: Marianne! Marianne! Hop in! I'll give you a ride.

(MARIANNE JOST, *thirty-five, stylish in short black hair and long black coat, steps closer, looks through the rain.*)

LETOUR: John. John LeTour.

MARIANNE: (*Recognizes him*) John?

LETOUR: Get in. You're getting soaked.

(*She ducks inside, slams the door.*)

MARIANNE: (*Awkward*) Hi . . .

(*The car moves on.*)

LETOUR: Where are you going?

(MARIANNE *wipes rain from her cheeks; her expression deepens: cautious, suspicious. No reply.*)

LETOUR: I didn't know you still lived here.

MARIANNE: (*Second thoughts*) Maybe this wasn't such a good idea. I should get out.

LETOUR: Don't be crazy. It's pouring.

MARIANNE: I'm not supposed to be around—

LETOUR: (*Completes sentence*)—former drug associates.

MARIANNE: It's four years I'm clean. No alcohol, no cigarettes, no nothing.

LETOUR: I heard. I'm happy for you.

MARIANNE: It's still not easy.

LETOUR: I know. Mar, you don't need to avoid me. I'm straight—two years. It came that time. I tried to tell you. I wrote. I called.

MARIANNE: (*Looks around*) I should get out.

LETOUR: Honest.

MARIANNE: But you're dealing.

LETOUR: No. I stopped.

MARIANNE: What's in the bag?

LETOUR: Almond oil. You can check. (*Opens bag.*) Look.
    (*She does: Enhancements Almond Oil. John's beeper goes off!—he punches it.*)

LETOUR: Shit.

MARIANNE: What's that for? In case someone needs almond oil in the middle of the night?

LETOUR: I still deal a little, but I'm straight – that part's true. Believe me.

MARIANNE: (*To* DRIVER) Stop here. Now. Stop!

LETOUR: I won't say anything. I promise. I'll just sit here. I'll just give you a ride.

(*The car pulls over.* MARIANNE *opens the door, gets out.*)

MARIANNE: Goodbye, John.

LETOUR: Where do you live? (*Door slams.*) Mari . . .

(*She fades into the rain.* JOHN *watches, aching.*)

DRIVER: Sir?

LETOUR: Eighty-third Street.

(*The sedan continues uptown.*)

CUT TO:

MEMORIES

John's apartment. Pre-dawn. His diary lies open on the desk.
LETOUR *sits clothed on the futon, drinking white wine. He pages through a cheap, half-filled photo album. He touches snapshots, 3x5's from another time:*

— JOHN *and* MARIANNE, *arm in arm, on a Florida beach*
— MARIANNE, *surprised by the camera, snorting coke at a party*
— JOHN, MARIANNE, *and* ANN *posing, smiling, same party*
— JOHN *and* MARIANNE *kissing over birthday cake, same party*
— MARIANNE *in Morocco bazaar*
— JOHN *blowing a kiss in Fez airport*

CUT TO:

PSYCHIC HEALING

LeTour's narration continues over embossed card on an entry table: Teresa Aronow, Psychic Reading, 37 Jones Street, New York, N.Y. 10012, (212)473–4297. VOICES *under narration:*

TERESA: (*Out of shot*) Coffee?

LETOUR: (*Out of shot*) Thanks.

TERESA: (*Out of shot*) Black?

15

LETOUR: (*Out of shot*) Yeah.

TERESA: (*Out of shot*) Here.

> (JOHN *accepts a coffee mug, sits on a sofa across from*
> TERESA. *Sunlight falls through crocheted curtains.*
> TERESA ARONOW, *fortyish, professionally young, is compact,*
> *demure; she wears business jacket and skirt, patterned blouse.*
> *Nothing about her is remotely paranormal—nothing except,*
> *of course, her "aura." The "Other Side." Her voice is at the*
> *same time soothing, piercing.*
> *Teresa's West Village consultation room is startlingly*
> *mundane: a bourgeois walk-up. Upholstered furniture,*
> *Tiffany objêts d'art, framed photos of her husband and*
> *children—a trip to Capri. A twenties portrait of Madame*
> *Blavatsky, above the fireplace, centers the room.*)

LETOUR: I'm not sure how this works.

TERESA: Have you ever been to a psychic before?

LETOUR: No, but I've, well, I've heard about it.

TERESA: Do you need advice? John?

LETOUR: (*Nods*) No . . . it's not that . . . I don't know—I
just decided to come. I thought . . .

TERESA: Be comfortable. (*Smile.*) How did you hear about me?

LETOUR: A recommendation. Somebody from work. Two hundred dollars, right?

(TERESA *nods.* JOHN *tucks cash into an envelope, places it on the coffee table.*)

TERESA: It's a lot of money?

LETOUR: I don't care.

TERESA: (*Explaining*) I look at you. I give you my impressions. I feel your "vibrations"—I don't like that word, it sounds phony, but I can't think of anything better. (*Watching.*) You're anxious.

(*He shrugs.*)

More than usual. Your aura is very strong. I feel a very strong vibration from you. A change is coming. You're worried about money. You say you don't care about money but that's not true.

LETOUR: Yeah.

TERESA: Your livelihood is endangered. You're worried about the future. You don't have much money saved. What will you do?

LETOUR: I don't know.

TERESA: I see a woman who has betrayed you.

LETOUR: (*Smiles*) My mother?

TERESA: (*Cuts him short*) Who *will* betray you.

LETOUR: Not . . . I . . .

TERESA: Keep it in mind. I have a strong feeling about this woman, a woman close to you, she will betray you. You're in the entertainment business, aren't you?

LETOUR: Yes.

TERESA: But you're not happy. You want to do something else. Is it music?

LETOUR: Yes . . .

TERESA: You have a talent for music.

LETOUR: As a child.

TERESA: You still have it. It's strong. I see music in your future. A career opportunity will come in the music field. Take it. It won't seem promising. Take it anyway. (*Pause.*) You're full of stress. Are you exercising?

LETOUR: No. I—

17

TERESA: You should exercise more. You must let go of this stress. It's not good for your health. I'm not saying you're going over to the other side, but it's not good for you. You're still drinking, aren't you? You have a drinking problem?

(*He shrugs.*)

It's interfering with your health and your life too. You've had other problems. Drug addiction.

LETOUR: Yes.

TERESA: This was very important in your life.

LETOUR: Yes.

TERESA: You are in the balance. Everything you do – positive or negative – in this life is a drop that will carry over in the next. Every act, every decision matters.

LETOUR: Teresa?

TERESA: What is it?

LETOUR: I'm thirty-eight years old. (*Beat.*) Forty.

TERESA: You're young.

LETOUR: I have trouble sleeping.

(TERESA *waits.*)

Look. What do you see around me? Is there anything? Is it dark? Have I run out of luck? Is there luck?

TERESA: I see a glow. Everything you need is around you. The only danger is inside you.

CUT TO:

MONEY CHANGER

Ann's apartment. The night has already begun. ANN *sits on the floor beside a* YOUNG HASID *counting money. He wears Orthodox garb: black hat, black coat, peyas. Tibetan bells reverb from speakers as the Bergmanesque cambist runs faced twenty-dollar bills through a battery-operated counting machine, places stacks of cash on the floor.* ROBERT *returns a call from the kitchen;* LETOUR *emerges from the bathroom, wiping his hands.*

ANN: (*To* LETOUR *and* ROBERT) Your pay's on the table.

(JOHN *walks to the cosmetics corner, finds an envelope with his name on it, looks inside: $500 in twenties. He pockets the money.*

18

LETOUR *sits as* HASID *double-checks the total: cash covers the available floor space.*)

YOUNG HASID: (*Dialogue punctuates action*) One hundred thirty-one, let's make it 130–$13,000, hundreds for small bills. One percent commission, $130 to you—add tens or whatever if you want.

(*Opening a satchel, he removes bound $100s, counts off 130 as* ANN *adds up commission in small bills. He loads the satchel:*)

YOUNG HASID: Same time?

ANN: (*Nods*) Two weeks—don't run. Stay a while. We'll order kosher. We'll tell you dirty stories. We'll talk Zionism.

(*The* HASID *laughs. He likes her.*)

YOUNG HASID: (*Passes hundreds*) I'm late already. I only come 'cause I like you. Sure you're not Jewish? I don't want to see you hurt. Find a man. You should do something else.

ANN: (*Offers commission*) Invest in my cosmetics line.

YOUNG HASID: (*Takes money*) Don't mix business with friendship.

(ANN *follows him to the door.*)

YOUNG HASID: Shalom.

ANN: Shalom. (*Opens door.*) See you next week. (*Calls after him.*) Don't eat any hot dogs!
(ANN *closes door.*)

LETOUR: Jealous said something about a yuppie murder in the Park. You know anything about it?

ANN: It's all over the news.

LETOUR: Jealous said to be careful.

ANN: We are careful.

ROBERT: (*Returning*) We're too small time. Besides, she wasn't one of ours—not directly.
(*To* LETOUR.)
Tis is at St. Luke's. He wants somebody over right away. Second floor waiting room.

LETOUR: A hospital? What's he doing there?

ROBERT: He says he needs you to come to St. Luke's. I'd go but I got the other thing.

LETOUR: The—?

ROBERT: Yeah.

ANN: (*To* LETOUR) Go. Keep on his good side. He set up Arizona.
(*Phone rings; Ann's machine answers: "Hello, this is Ann . . . "*)

ANN: (*To* LETOUR) Let's have lunch. Tomorrow.

LETOUR: Me?

ANN: One o'clock. Côte Basque. Is that too early?

LETOUR: No. Yeah—sure.

ROBERT: Tonight?

LETOUR: I vote Japanese.

ANN: Fine.

ROBERT: Okay.

LETOUR: (*Heads for door*) Mixed sushi. Oshitashi.

CUT TO:

ST. LUKE'S

EMS vehicles line street outside St. Luke's–Roosevelt Hospital. Inside, LETOUR *weaves through Emergency (eerie), double-steps the stairs, looks for the second floor waiting area.*
TIS (*Mathis—pronounced Tees*), *thirty-five, Swiss, paces in the*

waiting room. He wears a linen jacket, horn-rim glasses, Cerrutti
Euro-swank. He spots JOHN, *takes him aside:*

LETOUR: What's going on?

TIS: You got some valiums?

LETOUR: (*Nods*) —'n 'ludes.

TIS: Just a valium—a ten.

LETOUR: What is it?

TIS: You won't believe it. What a nightmare. I brought in this chick. She O.D.ed—man, I didn't even know her. I didn't have to bring her in. The cops are coming back to talk to me. I'm hyper. I gotta come down.

LETOUR: (*Hands him valium*) Here.

TIS: Make it two.

(LETOUR *obliges.* TIS *pops a blue without water, pockets the other.*)

TIS: Thanks.

LETOUR: She okay?

TIS: Who?

LETOUR: The girl.

TIS: Yeah, yeah. Met her last night. A walking vacuum cleaner. What a nightmare. Underage.

LETOUR: You need a lawyer?

TIS: (*Gestures toward suited man*) He's here. Thanks.

(TIS *folds a bill into John's hand.*)

LETOUR: Any time.

(TIS *turns, steps away.* LETOUR *walks down the long corridor. Curious, reflective, he slows past open doors. Friends, family, patients sit in blue light. Each room a drama.*

He heads down a duplicate corridor. A VOICE *turns his head:*)

RANDI: John!

(*He turns to see* RANDI JOST, *thirty, Marianne's younger sister. She wears running shoes, jeans, red sweater.*)

LETOUR: Randi?

RANDI: (*Kisses him*) I can't believe it. Marianne's here too. She flew in. It's been so long. You look great.

LETOUR: (*Deactivates beeper*) You too. Randi, what's wrong? Why are you here?

21

RANDI: Mom. She's back in. Didn't Marianne tell you?

LETOUR: Serious?

RANDI: (*Nods*) More chemo.

LETOUR: Can I see her?

RANDI: She's sleeping. She sleeps most of the time. She'd like it, though. She still talks about you.

LETOUR: (*Sad*) I'm so sorry. She's a terrific woman. I was crazy about her. God.

(MARIANNE, *head down, approaches. Looking up, she finds herself unexpectedly beside* JOHN *and* RANDI:)

RANDI: It's John. What a coincidence.

MARIANNE: (*Gathering herself*) Yes. (*Extends hand.*) Hi.

LETOUR: (*Shakes hand*) Randi told me about your mom. I'm sorry.

MARIANNE: Thanks.

LETOUR: She's sedated?

MARIANNE: Yeah.

RANDI: She would be so happy to see John.

MARIANNE: I don't think that would be a good idea.

(*An awkward silence:* RANDI *doesn't get it.*)

LETOUR: You both look so tired.

MARIANNE: One of us has to be here.

RANDI: The hospital lets us stay in her room.

LETOUR: Let me buy you some coffee or something – the cafeteria's downstairs. It helps to talk.

RANDI: You go, Marianne, it's my turn with mom.

MARIANNE: I shouldn't.

RANDI: Go. You haven't eaten. Go on. (*Nudges her.*) Go on.

MARIANNE: I . . .

RANDI: Bring me a coffee.

(MARIANNE *acquiesces.*)

LETOUR: This way.

(*To* RANDI.)

Kiss your mother for me.

(JOHN *escorts* MARIANNE *toward the stairs.*)

CUT TO:

EUPHORIC RECALL

Hospital cafeteria. JOHN *and* MARIANNE *carry trays to a formica table, molded chairs. He mixes sugar in his coffee as she sets out her salad, diet soda, to-go coffee.*

An awkward moment. MARIANNE *scans the fluorescent room: doctors, nurses, relatives.*

LETOUR: I like your mom.

MARIANNE: She liked you. You know this will happen someday, but when it does . . . Your mother – *that* was a shock.

LETOUR: (*Re: Marianne's mother*) She's been sick a while?

MARIANNE: A year.

LETOUR: Your father?

MARIANNE: (*"No"*) Not this time. His new wife – he'll make it to the funeral.

LETOUR: What have you been doing? Where do you live?

MARIANNE: It's . . . (*Deciding.*) I don't want you to know about my life.

LETOUR: Anything? You married? Have children? A dog? (*Smile.*) House plants?

23

MARIANNE: Details just open the door.

LETOUR: The door to what?

(*No answer.*)

It's not like we're strangers. We were married.

MARIANNE: We were not.

LETOUR: There was a ceremony.

MARIANNE: He wasn't even a minister. He was an astrologer.

LETOUR: He was also a minister. "Universal Harmony."

MARIANNE: He was a Pisces.

LETOUR: You're a Pisces.

MARIANNE: It was *not* legal.

LETOUR: In the eyes of Jeanne Dixon we're still—

MARIANNE: I was on the cusp.

LETOUR: We were happy.

MARIANNE: We were miserable. We were either scoring or coming down—mostly coming down.

LETOUR: There were good times. Area, out on the street, laughing, dancing with friends—we were *magical*.

MARIANNE: You took off for three months without telling me and called once. That's how magical we were. You were an encyclopedia of suicidal fantasies—I heard them all. Nobody could clear a room like you, John. And the friends, you may have noticed, turned out to be mine, not yours. I envy you. A convenient memory is a gift from God.

LETOUR: You exaggerate.

MARIANNE: In rehab they call this "euphoric recall." You only remember the highs, never the lows.

LETOUR: We were happy.

MARIANNE: I was drowning.

LETOUR: It wasn't me—

MARIANNE: You watched—

LETOUR: You jumped—

MARIANNE: You did nothing—"It wasn't your business, you weren't responsible"—you still think like that. (*Shakes head.*) Actions have consequences; so do—

LETOUR: (*Overlap*) I—

MARIANNE: —inactions.

LETOUR: I didn't—

(MARIANNE *smiles.*)

I meant well.

MARIANNE: You always meant well.

LETOUR: We *were* in love?

MARIANNE: Yes.

LETOUR: We *were* happy?

(*She doesn't answer. He slides his hand across the table. She notices his gold and onyx ring.*)

LETOUR: You bought it for me. It's inscribed inside.

(*She pushes his hand away. Details open doors.*)

LETOUR: Ann's quitting. I've got to find something else to do.

MARIANNE: Ann? I'll believe it when I see it.

LETOUR: It's true.

MARIANNE: Are you really straight?

LETOUR: Yeah.

MARIANNE: Let me see your eyes.

(JOHN *leans forward, eyes open. She presses up an eyelid, examines one iris, the other:*)

MARIANNE: Eyes are deceiving. (*Beat.*) Congratulations.

LETOUR: If I could do that, I could do anything.

MARIANNE: What do you mean?

LETOUR: *We* could do anything. We could start over.

MARIANNE: (*Bangs her head*) What was that? I think I heard something.

LETOUR: I'm serious.

(*An* INTERCOM VOICE *announces visiting hours will end in five minutes.*)

MARIANNE: You're crazy.

LETOUR: (*Gestures to room*) *This* is crazy.

MARIANNE: I have to get back.

(JOHN *nods, checks his watch—he's late too. They exchange "last looks"*; MARIANNE *stands.*)

LETOUR: I'll walk you.

(*He stands, follows.*)

CUT TO:

NEW DIARY

Later. LeTour's sedan pulls up near Palio, a midtown restaurant. JOHN *steps around garbage bags, enters.*

Inside, JOHN *"maps" bar, greets the* MAÎTRE D'. LETOUR *spots the* FRENCH (*LaCroix and Montana*) COUPLE *in the dining section, catches the man's eye. He nods to the* MAÎTRE D', *makes his way toward their table.*

He joins the FRENCH COUPLE, *declines a drink, exchanges drugs/money amid air kisses.*

Late night. Fog hangs over 22nd Street: Chelsea's deserted. Homeless men behind windbreaks of trash.

John's apartment. He writes bareback at the desk. He completes his composition book diary mid-sentence, closes it, discards it. He lifts a new book from the floor, opens it on the desk, continues. He fills his glass with wine:

LETOUR: (*Voice over*) I can always find another way to make a living. I never planned this in the first place—not like Ann. She came up to sell, have parties, make contacts. She was so glamorous. I just wanted to be around her. She'd sit up listening to coke stories. Now it's me and Robert. The whole crowd was the same age. Everybody's younger now. She made me.

(LETOUR *pulls his weekly pay from his pants, puts five twenties in an envelope. He addresses the envelope. "Linda*

26

Wichel, 1012B-2 A Street, Sacramento, California,"
stamps it.
Dissolves: (1) LETOUR *vanishes from his desk, (2)*
materializes fetally on his futon, bareback, slacks, boots,
anxious, awaiting sleep.
LeTour's diary contains parallel columns of names: one
headed "People Who Are Left Handed," the other, "People
Whose Eyes Don't Match.")

CUT TO:

CÔTE BASQUE

Midday. JOHN, *wearing a black tweed jacket, tie, khaki slacks,*
mails the Sacramento letter, enters CÔTE BASQUE, *a hoity-toity*
55th Street restaurant.
Midmeal. ANN *and* LETOUR *sit in a prominent booth; power*
moguls confer quietly. A deferential WAITER *brings fresh berries,*
retrieves empty salmon plates.

ANN: You have any money saved?

LETOUR: There's some. Not much. A thousand or two. Maybe
more—I'm not sure.

ANN: What do you do with your money?
(*The* CHEF *stops by, asks if the meal was satisfactory.* ANN
assures him it was, kisses his hand. The CHEF *nods, gratified.*
JOHN *resumes the conversation:*)

LETOUR: I don't know. It's not that much in the first place—as
you know.

ANN: (*Counterpoint*) It's tax free—

LETOUR: Rent, utilities, phone, tips, CDs—what about your
money?

ANN: Kitty Ford once told me, "Ann, the only person I know
that lives as well as you is my grandmother." All the
money I've made, all the money I've spent—it never adds
up. This last two years cosmetics' been taking everything.

LETOUR: I wish I could help.

ANN: You still go to meetings?

LETOUR: No, but I'm okay. What are the odds of meeting
someone you haven't seen in years twice in two days?

ANN: Ask Robert to make up a chart for you; the other
    person – who is it?
LETOUR: Just a contact – you don't know him.
ANN: What's the plan?
LETOUR: The plan?
ANN: What you gonna do?
LETOUR: My future?
ANN: Too conceptual?
LETOUR: We had this conversation two years ago. We'll have
    it two years from now.
ANN: This time it's for real.
LETOUR: (*Accepting premise*) I'm thinking of some music
    courses. Mixing, sound editing –
ANN: You took that before.
LETOUR: That was acting.
ANN: (*Corrects him*) Modeling.
LETOUR: Why all this concern? Suddenly you care?
ANN: I have feelings too – you may have noticed. I guess I'm
    worried. I'm tough, you gotta to be tough, especially in
    this business, it's one thing to act tough – I've seen
    Zipporah twice this week.

LETOUR: She helps you?

ANN: (*Nods*) —harmonizes, she's encouraging me to get out of
this into the cosmetics thing—
(WAITER *leans in, deposits check as* WELL-TANNED
CUSTOMER, *fifty-five, cologne and hauteur, passes. He looks
at* ANN *blankly, continues. She watches:*)

ANN: (*About* CUSTOMER) Nomination for Best Picture. I knew
every girl he fucked—how, why. I knew when he had
trouble shitting. Like this. (*Crosses fingers.*) His wife says
he gets straight or she cuts him off. Old money. I
remember the last thing he said to me: "See you soon."
Yeah, sure. That was five years ago.
(ANN *pulls a wad of twenties from her purse, counts bills
atop the check: $260.*)

ANN: (*Vulnerable*) You'll still talk to me, won't you?
(*A beat: this is the reason for lunch. The* WAITER *picks up
the cash, appraises the gratuity.*)

LETOUR: You—?
(*To* ANN.)
Of course I will.

ANN: It'll be strange without you around. I hadn't thought of
it—it hit me.

LETOUR: (*Clever*) We'll always have Paris.

ANN: (*Reproachful*) John.
(JOHN *reaches, touches her visceral emotion. He takes her
hand:*)

LETOUR: Ann, you want me, call, write a letter, tell a wino—
I'll be there.
(*She smiles, clasps his hand. Touching, he is touched.*)

CUT TO:

GENERAL HOSPITAL

Afternoon. St. Luke's. LETOUR, *wearing tweed jacket, walks
down the corridor, checks room numbers. A* NURSE *passes.
He stops at a room, pushes the door a crack, peeks inside, quietly
enters.*
Inside the hospital room, MRS. JOST, *sixty-five, lies sedated,
attached to IV tubes and a respirator. Flowers wreathe the bed.*

29

RANDI *sleeps in a chair by the window.*

LETOUR *looks from* MRS. JOST *to* RANDI *and back again: a vibrant woman reduced to a shell. He soundlessly eases into a vacant chair.*

His mind goes back.

RANDI *twists fitfully in her chair. A stuffed bear peeks over family photos on the window sill.*

MARIANNE *steps into the doorway, stops, frozen—watching the tableau:* JOHN, RANDI, *her mother. Her face is ravaged: the death watch has taken its toll.* LETOUR *reaches his arm, touches the hospital bed.*

MARIANNE *tiptoes behind* JOHN. *He turns, stands.*

LETOUR: (*Soft*) I'm sorry. I . . .
> (*She puts her finger to her lips. He nods. She steps closer, holds him politely. His cheek nestles in her neck.*
> *They turn toward the door, step into the corridor, walk arm in arm as if supporting each other.*)

LETOUR: (*After a moment*) I always thought my father would die first. He would die, then my mother and I would reconcile. Just her and me. I hated him for living.

MARIANNE: It's like a joke. It's not a real feeling. It's like a feeling of a feeling.

LETOUR: My old man bawling in the hospital, me popping in and out of the john getting loaded. (*Beat.*) I miss you.
> (*They stop. She kisses him.*)

MARIANNE: You tried to kill me. You took ten years of my life one way or another.
> (*He kisses her.*)
> I couldn't hate my mom—I was too busy hating you.

LETOUR: I thought I was just killing myself.
> (*She runs her hands under his shirt, up his back.*)

LETOUR: Selfish.

MARIANNE: I remember.

LETOUR: What?

MARIANNE: What it felt like. (*Kisses his face.*) What this tasted like.
> (*He slips his hands under her blouse, caresses her breasts.*)

LETOUR: I see you and my heart starts thumping.

MARIANNE: John.

(They kiss deeper, bodies grinding. The painful present fades. A NURSE *approaches with* WHEELCHAIR PATIENT. *She tries to pass one side of* JOHN *and* MARIANNE, *tries the other side, is blocked again. The* NURSE *stops, stares at their soap opera.*
Sensing her glare, JOHN *and* MARIANNE, *hands over and under each other, stop, look to the* NURSE: *embarrassed—yet blissful.)*
LETOUR: Excuse us.
(*To* MARIANNE.)
Let's go.
MARIANNE: Come. Come with me.

CUT TO:

HOTEL SEX

Paramount hotel room: Vermeer's Lace Maker *dominates Phillipe Stark decor.*
LETOUR *and* MARIANNE *are all over each other. The pain of the*

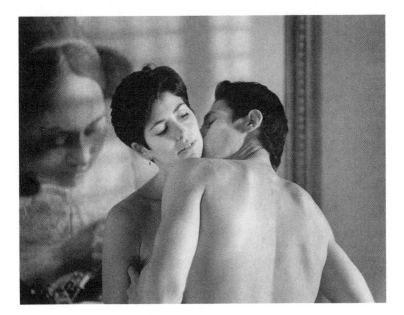

moment, the pain of the past are subsumed by passion. Blind, welcome sexuality.

Naked, they kneel facing each other on the bed, faded bleeding heart tattoo on his bicep:

LETOUR: Have you ever had sex totally straight?

MARIANNE: Not with you.

LETOUR: Neither have I.

MARIANNE: Such an erection.

LETOUR: Never had anything like it stoned. Feel it.

    (*She does.*)

MARIANNE: Weird.

LETOUR: (*Caresses erection*) Wow.

MARIANNE: I'm dripping.

LETOUR: Let's disappear.

    (*They smack their sweaty bodies, tumble yelping to the carpet, kiss indiscriminately:*)

LETOUR: Kiss, kiss, kiss.

MARIANNE: Kiss, kiss, kiss.

LETOUR: Together.

    (*Later: night. They lie nude in a scramble of twisted sheets and mattresses. Street lights cast horizontal shadows.*

    LETOUR *crawls over, falls upon Marianne's breast. She wakes up, looks at* JOHN, *looks out the window, returns to slow sad reality.*

    MARIANNE *stands, pulls on her panties.*)

LETOUR: (*Waking*) You need to go back?

    (*She dresses before responding:*)

MARIANNE: This is the end. It was wonderful. I'm glad it happened this way. It will never happen again. You will not see me, you will not call me again. I'm happy for you. I wish you the best. I'm leaving. I'm going back to the hospital. I shouldn't have left—but I don't regret it. Please dress and leave as soon as possible. I have a key. Goodbye.

LETOUR: Marianne . . .

MARIANNE: It's my fault.

    (MARIANNE, *clothes askew, exits.*)

LETOUR: I love you.

    (LETOUR *is alone. He pulls his pants on. Looking for his socks, he peruses Marianne's personal things. He examines her cosmetics, her underclothes. He dabs her perfume on his cheek.*

Buttoning his shirt, he retrieves his beeper from suit jacket. Activated, it disgorges messages. He checks his watch: 9:00 p.m.)

CUT TO:

GET ON OUT

Nine-thirty: Ann's apartment building. Trash stacked high.

LETOUR *presses the buzzer.*

LETOUR, *exhausted, unfocused, enters Ann's apartment.* ANN *is immediately upon him:*

ANN: Johnny, what is this? Your beeper broke, gettin' some shiatsu? Two hours: where have you been?

LETOUR: There was a mix-up—

ANN: How you gonna survive on your own? The U.N.'s got some conference in two days. The holiday's over— ragheads everywhere trying to score. U.N. security at every hotel—little creeps with lapel pins. Even I've been out. This is where our money is: Europe, Asia, not the streets—you wouldn't know crack from crackerjacks.

LETOUR: Where's Robert?

ANN: Busting his ass. He's out doing your job.

LETOUR: It was a confusion.

ANN: Get confused on your day off.

LETOUR: When is that?

ANN: Don't get wise. What do you want me to do? Suck your dick?—okay. A raise? No way. Get out there. There's a list on the TV. I love you. Get your ass outta here before I kiss it.

LETOUR: (*Pecks her cheek*) I'm on my way. Love you. Forgive me.

CUT TO:

AU BAR

LeTour's sedan waits between limos.

Inside, JOHN *passes the* MAÎTRE D', *looks around: he's known*

33

*here. Au Bar, a restaurant/club open 9:00 p.m. to 4:00 a.m.,
caters to the young, the rich, the European.*
He spots TIS *with* THOMAS, *twenty-five, his handsome trainer,
and* TWO MODELS *at a second-floor table. They exchange nods.*
LETOUR *scans the room: suspicion is second nature.*
*A laughing man (*GUIDONE*) at the bar catches his eye. He seems
to blend: Italian, twenty-eight, silk suit, impeccable hair, accent —
but something's not right. His black shoes have rubber soles.*
LETOUR *looks for a gun bulge, dirty hands. The* ITALIAN *turns;*
LETOUR *glimpses his face: too pale. The* ITALIAN *averts his eyes.*
Glancing back, LETOUR *walks up the stairs to Tis' table.*

TIS: Tour, sit. Take a rest. LeTour, this is Gabri, Tasha — you
    know Thomas. They're here for a show.
    (*The* MODELS *respond in respective accents.* THOMAS *extends
    his hand.* JOHN *shakes, remains standing.*)

LETOUR: Enchanté.
    (*To* TIS.)
    How'd it turn out?

TIS: (*To* GABRI) Questo è un vero *Americano*.
    (*To* LETOUR.)
    What?
    (GABRI *and* TASHA *buzz.*)

LETOUR: St. Luke's.

TIS: No problem, but — can you believe this? — she's out of the
    hospital in one day, calls me up, wants to "get together."
    Some people are just born for losing. Want to go in back?

LETOUR: Not now.

TIS: Huh?

LETOUR: Look at the bar. Black-haired guy, late twenties,
    brown suit, drinking tonic?
    (TIS *nods.*)
    He's casing you. Not me, you. Undercover, whatever —
    he's on you.

TIS: You know him?

LETOUR: (*Shakes head "no"*) Just a feeling. You holding?

TIS: No. Need help?

LETOUR: (*"No"*) Leave a message. Robert or I will come by
    later.

TIS: Forget it. It wasn't for me anyway.

(*To* MODELS.)

Who am I trying to impress?

(*They smile uncomprehendingly.*)

Make it tomorrow. A half—no, three-quarters.

LETOUR: Nineteen is the top. I'll make two trips.

TIS: Nineteen is fine.

LETOUR: (*Leaving*) A domani. Take care, girls.

CUT TO:

THERE IS A DIRECTION

The blue sedan drives west past Times Square, turns north on Eighth Ave. A plastic wall of trash stretches toward the river. Port Authority hustlers—male, female—cruise as TRANSIT COPS *whack an emaciated* CRACKHEAD. JOHN, *lit by neon, lowers his power window.*

John's apartment. Night. He writes in his diary, drinks.

LETOUR: (*Voice over*) I feel my life turning. All it needed was a direction. You drift from day to day, years go by. Suddenly there is a direction. What a strange thing to happen halfway through your life.

(*He goes to the phone, dials. A voice answers:*)

HOTEL SWITCHBOARD: (*Out of shot*) Paramount Hotel.

LETOUR: Marianne Jost, please.

HOTEL SWITCHBOARD: (*Out of shot*) Just a moment.

(*A pre-recorded message comes on:*)

HOTEL MESSAGE: "Welcome to the Paramount. Your party is out. If you would like to leave a message for— (*Marianne's voice*) 'Marianne Jost' (*back to message*) —please do so after the beep."

(LETOUR *hangs up, carries the phone to the boombox. He dials again, presses 'Record,' holds the receiver to the mike, records the hotel message, hangs up.*

First light slants from the window. LETOUR *lies clothed on the futon, boombox by his ear. He presses "Play" and "Rewind," running the tape over and over, listening, re-listening to Marianne's voice: "Marianne Jost." "Marianne Jost." "Marianne Jost."*)

35

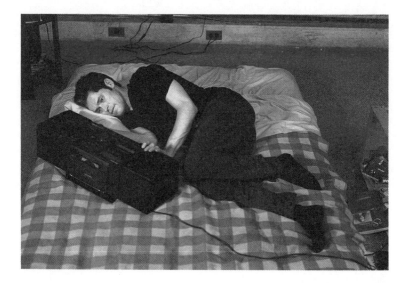

CUT TO:

PHONE CALLS

*Midday. Twenty-second Street. A helter-skelter of daytime
activity unseen before.*
John's apartment. Sunlight fills the studio apartment. LETOUR,
*unshaven in T-shirt and slacks, sets the phone on the desk beside
his open composition book. He pauses, dials.*
HOTEL SWITCHBOARD: (*Out of shot*) Paramount Hotel.
LETOUR: Marianne Jost.
HOTEL SWITCHBOARD: (*Out of shot*) Just a moment.
   (JOHN *waits, closes his diary.*)
HOTEL SWITCHBOARD: (*Out of shot*) I'm sorry. Ms. Jost
   checked out this morning.
LETOUR: She was there yesterday.
HOTEL SWITCHBOARD: (*Out of shot*) She checked out this
   morning.
LETOUR: Did she leave a forwarding number?
HOTEL SWITCHBOARD: (*Out of shot*) No.
LETOUR: Thank you.
   (*He hangs up, thinks, redials.*)

ST. LUKE'S SWITCHBOARD: (*Out of shot*) St. Luke's–Roosevelt
Hospital.
LETOUR: Mrs. Jost. JoAnn Jost. She's a patient.
ST. LUKE'S SWITCHBOARD: (*Out of shot*) Just a moment.
(*A long silence.* JOHN *looks out the window. A* MEDICAL
STAFF VOICE *from the hospital:*)
MEDICAL VOICE: (*Out of shot*) Who is this calling?
LETOUR: (*Thinking*) Skyline Floral. We're trying to confirm a
delivery.
MEDICAL VOICE: (*Out of shot*) Mrs. Jost passed away last night.
LETOUR: Are the funeral arrangements local?
MEDICAL VOICE: (*Out of shot*) Just a sec – yes, Plaza Memorial.
LETOUR: Thank you.
MEDICAL VOICE: (*Out of shot*) You're welcome.
(JOHN *hangs up, paces, sits.*)

CUT TO:

DIRTY LAUNDRY

*Afternoon. Chelsea laundromat. Mothers and maids gossip, sort
clothes. Hispanic radio underscores the whirl of machines.*
LETOUR, *unshaven, shoves dirty clothes into a washer. He counts
out quarters, starts the machine.*
Heading toward a vacant chair, he spots a MAN *out the window.
It takes a second to place the face: it's the "Italian" from Au Bar
in street clothes. He watches* JOHN *watching him.*
LETOUR *walks outside, approaches* GUIDONE *on the sidewalk:*
LETOUR: Can I help you, officer?
GUIDONE: What?
LETOUR: I hope I haven't made a mistake. You are a cop,
aren't you?
GUIDONE: Yes.
LETOUR: Could I see a badge?
(GUIDONE *eyes* LETOUR *with disdain: the contempt of a cop
for a dealer, of youth for middle age.*)
GUIDONE: (*Shows credentials*) Bill Guidone.
LETOUR: What is it?
GUIDONE: You think you're invisible, don't you? You think we
don't know you, LeTour – that's the name you use, right?

37

LETOUR: My father's a partner in a powerful law firm. If you have anything in mind, do it by the book.
(GUIDONE *elbow-stabs* LETOUR, *kicks his shin. Wincing, retreating,* JOHN staggers, *regains his balance.*)

GUIDONE: (*In his face*) You? Who the fuck cares about you? I could grind you right here!—maybe I will!—and nobody would give a fuck! You're not worth the paperwork. I look like Narcotics? I'm Homicide—I'm investigating the Park murder.

LETOUR: (*Acquiescent*) I don't follow the news.

GUIDONE: Downtown's interested how a Barnard honors student with fancy parents got a quarter of uncut coke on her when she was murdered. I mean, we just don't see this girl cruising Alphabet City trying to score. Somebody sold her, somebody upscale and classy—you're classy, I hear—and that somebody knows something we need to know. (*Hand inside LeTour's shirt, pinching his tit.*) Delivery boy!

LETOUR: I wish I could help. I don't even know who's president.

GUIDONE: Let me put it this way. Here's my card (*Hands card.*) Ask around, take a week or so. Call me. Tell me

something I don't know. Either that, leave town, or get
your ass busted day in, day out.
(LETOUR *examines the card.*)

CUT TO:

FUNERAL HOME

Evening. LETOUR, *shaven, in black tweed jacket, white shirt,
black tie, crosses Amsterdam Avenue, enters Plaza Memorial
Chapel.*
Inside funeral home, JOHN *checks the letterboard for Mrs. Jost's
name. An arrow directs him.*
Nondenominational muzak. Senior citizens whisper off-screen.
Walking, he sees MARIANNE, *dressed in black. She sees him, turns
to him; her face hollow, desperate:*
MARIANNE: Get out.
LETOUR: Marianne . . .
MARIANNE: (*Emotion rising*) Every time you come into my life
    something terrible happens. I thought I was rid of you.
    How'd you get here? I don't want you here! I don't want
    you around me, I don't want you around my mother!
    Damn you!
LETOUR: Marianne . . .
MARIANNE: (*Wild*) Get out!
    (*A* PLAZA MEMORIAL EMPLOYEE *approaches.* RANDI, *in
    black, intervenes, pulls* JOHN *toward the door.* MARIANNE
    YELLS *from behind: "Out!" Outside, they stop mid-
    sidewalk.*)
LETOUR: I didn't . . .
RANDI: I'm sorry. That's the way it is. You shouldn't have
    come. Marianne has been up all night, crying and crying.
    She wasn't there when Mother passed—died—she blames
    herself. It wouldn't have made any difference. She just
    slipped away. Marianne's—I'm worried—
    (*A* CRACKHEAD *strides past trash ramparts, cursing,
    demanding money: "Fuck white devil, fucking the black, give
    the fucking money, white fuck . . . ," etc.*)
LETOUR: It's . . .
RANDI: Don't try.

LETOUR: How are *you*?

RANDI: Me?

LETOUR: Yes, you. I can't think of anything, but if there was anything I could do . . .

RANDI: Thanks. I'm okay—I guess. I mean, we've been expecting it. It'll hit me later.

LETOUR: I saw her.

RANDI: Who?

LETOUR: Your mother. I came in the room. You were sleeping. I just watched.

RANDI: Oh. (*Beat.*) I'd better get back. Marianne's probably flipping out.

(*She re-enters the funeral chapel.*)

CUT TO:

ON A ROLL

Eight p.m. LETOUR, *direct from Plaza Memorial, enters Ann's apartment.* ANN, *coiffured and made up, gestures to take-out tins:*

ANN: Have some shu mai. Just delivered.

LETOUR: No.

ROBERT: (*Entering*) I told Ann you'd be on time. Tis called. He said before ten. He said you were right.

ANN: About what?

LETOUR: An undercover cop. Not a narc. The Park murder. Jealous was straight on that—you hear anything?

ROBERT: Remember the time that cop called here? Wanted to know if we had "nose candy"? (*Laughs.*) Ann says, "John Candy?" "John Candy?"

(ANN *looks at* JOHN, *approaches:*)

ANN: What's wrong baby? You like like shit. Something wrong? (*Holds his face.*)

LETOUR: No.

ANN: You can't fool me. I can read you.

LETOUR: (*Distressed*) What do you care? You're leaving me. A few more months—sayonara.

(*To* ROBERT.)

You too. John who? What was his name again? Le—?

40

(*To* ANN: *pained.*)
I mean it's not exactly like I got a pension plan.
ROBERT: (*Hurt*) Jack.
ANN: (*Takes his hands*) Johnny, it's not that at all. Is that what you think? You *hate* cosmetics. You don't care about it. You *told* me that.
LETOUR: I know.
ANN: Who knows what will happen?
ROBERT: I got a friend—a D.D.—got into lapidary. I'll introduce you. You have to pass a test.
LETOUR: Lapi—?
ROBERT: Gems, you know, crystals, diamonds.
LETOUR: Any more about the Park murder?
ANN: (*Re: murder*) What's with this thing?
ROBERT: Stay away.
ANN: (*Genuine*) You want in? We'll make a place for you.
LETOUR: No.
ANN: It's—
(*The kitchen phone rings. A voice follows the pre-recorded message:*)
EDDIE: (*Out of shot—answering machine*) "Ann, this is Ed. You gotta come. The other thing is over. I'll be home all night. 749-2876."
ROBERT: Shit.
ANN: (*Unequivocal*) Don't answer it. Let him call all night. He's trouble. I don't want to deal with him.
LETOUR: It's alright, I'll go. Let me handle it.
ROBERT: I'm sorry if—
ANN: (*About* EDDIE) He gives you shit—fuck him.
LETOUR: (*To* ROBERT) Forget it.
ROBERT: We're going Chinese tonight, okay? I mean we're on a roll—
ANN: Spring roll.
LETOUR: (*Preparing to leave*) Sure, whatever. Surprise me.

41

INTERVENTION

Eddie's high-rise apartment. EDDIE *is worse, if anything. He's been scoring on the street: broken pipes and vials crunch underfoot.*

EDDIE *and* LETOUR *argue (*"Fuck you!" "Fuck you!"*).* EDDIE *spits, pushes* TOUR, JOHN *pushes back. Eddie's feet tangle. He trips, FALLS. A bottle SMASHES.*

JOHN *goes to the phone, checks Eddie's directory, dials.*

EDDIE: (*On floor*) You gotta get permission? Check with Mama?

LETOUR: I'm calling your brother.

EDDIE: Huh?

LETOUR: Yeah, the lawyer in Bronxville. I'm gonna ask him to come over.

(EDDIE *protests.*)

You've told me so much about him.

EDDIE: (*Panicked*) No, don't. Please, I'll give you money, anything. He doesn't understand. Whose side are you on?

LETOUR: (*On phone*) Is this Martin Jeer? (*Beat.*) Thank you.

(EDDIE, *woozy, tries to stand.*)

EDDIE: I shoulda never called.

LETOUR: (*To* EDDIE) I recommend Hazelden. It has the best all-around program.

(*On phone.*) Martin Jeer? (*Beat.*) I'm here with your brother Ed. (*Beat.*) Yeah, in the city. I'm afraid there's a medical emergency. You're going to have to come.

(EDDIE *lurches toward* LETOUR. JOHN — *flash of anger* — *boot-kicks him in the head! Eddie's cheek hits the carpet.*)

LETOUR: (*On phone*) He'll be here.

(JOHN, *cooling down, measures his breaths. A spring can only be wound so tight.*)

CUT TO:

LEXINGTON AVENUE

LETOUR *walks from his sedan around the corner to the Lexington Avenue entrance to Grace Towers, a pre-war apartment building.*

In the lobby, he gives his name to the SECURITY GUARD, *is directed to the express elevator.*

He exits on the thirtieth floor; footsteps muted by thick carpet. Victorian prints on dark blue walls. He looks about, approaches a door, presses the buzzer.

THOMAS *opens the door;* JOHN *enters Tis' opulent apartment. Salle and Clemente hang on the walls; New York twinkles outside panoramic windows. A pipe and syringe lie atop art books.*

TIS, *in jogging sweats, comes from the bedroom to greet him.*

TIS: Tour, just in time. We were out. Nineteen, right?

LETOUR: Thirty-eight hundred – got any hundreds?

TIS: Some, not the whole thing.

   (*To* THOMAS.)

   You got hundreds?

THOMAS: No.

   (LETOUR *hands him a plastic bag of gram envelopes.* TIS *opens a packet, pours the contents on the coffee table.*)

TIS: I like that about Ann. Always takes the time to grind it. If you do it, do it right.

(JOHN *hears footsteps, turns to see* MARIANNE *stumble out of the bedroom! She looks terrible: shoeless, blouse out, hair undone, bruise on her forehead—perhaps she fell against something—hands trembling.*)

TIS: (*To* MARIANNE) Looks like you could use some help.

(MARIANNE *looks up, sees* JOHN, *goes pale.*)

Mari, this is Tour. You got any hundreds?

(JOHN *stares speechless: the girl who won't talk to him because he's a dealer.* MARIANNE *bolts back into the bedroom, SLAMS the door!*)

Not the talkative type. Haven't seen her in years. You know her, don't you?

(*No answer.* TIS *counts the money, offers it.* LETOUR *is frozen.*)

Why they call me? What a nightmare. (*Extending money.*) You want it or not?

LETOUR: (*Vacant*) Yeah.

(LETOUR *pockets the cash.* TIS, *his arm on John's elbow, "walks" him to the door:*)

TIS: See you later.

(TIS *nudges* JOHN *to the corridor, closes the door behind him.* JOHN *looks toward the elevator;* TIS, *behind the door, calls* "Marianne!"

Time cut: LETOUR *stands in the elevator, red floor numbers flashing past, blank eyes mirrored in dark glass.*)

CUT TO:

FALL FROM GRACE

JOHN *exits Grace Towers, walks past a limo toward Lexington Avenue. Rounding the corner, he sees his blue sedan. He looks at the cash, repockets it. He continues slowly, each step a separate task.*

LETOUR *reaches for the door handle. A scream pierces traffic noise. A car screeches, another. Voices call out.*

LETOUR *steps back, listens. He retraces his steps, turns onto Lexington Avenue. The* SECURITY GUARD, *walkie-talkie in hand, clusters on the sidewalk with the limo driver, two pedestrians. A cabbie jumps from his taxi, joins the confusion ("My God!"). A siren approaches. John's beeper goes off.*

Drawing closer, LETOUR *sees the partial bloodied shape of a broken body on the sidewalk: he recognizes Marianne's skirt.*

A squad car brakes with a screech. TWO COPS *converge, climb over trash, clear the crime scene:*

FEMALE COP: Get back!

MALE COP: Who saw it? What happened?

> (*The* FEMALE COP *bends over Marianne's body.*)
> EMS is on the way.

FEMALE COP: Too late —

> (*A second squad car pulls up.* JOHN *turns away, walks around the corner.*
> LETOUR *opens the car door, closes it, sits inside. A wailing ambulance flashes past, speeds up Central Park West.*
> LETOUR *doesn't react. Beeper re-beeps; he disconnects the battery.*
> *The driver,* CARLOS, *twenty-five, Hispanic, shirt starched, turns, looks, thinks, says:*)

CARLOS: Where to?

LETOUR: What?

CARLOS: Where to, sir? Where are we going?

LETOUR: Nowhere just now. Wait.

CARLOS: (*After a moment*) You want me to wait here?

LETOUR: Yes.

> (*Pause. More police cars. The EMS siren starts up; the ambulance speeds downtown past LeTour's sedan. No reaction.* CARLOS *turns off the engine.*)
> Downtown.

CARLOS: Yes.

> (CARLOS *starts the car, pulls into traffic.*)

CUT TO:

TWENTY-TWO MINUTES

John's apartment. Late night. LETOUR, *barefoot, T-shirt, slacks, stands flat against the wall.*

WINS broadcasts twenty-four hour news on the boombox. ("Give

us twenty-two minutes and we'll give you the world.") Sports, ads,
bullshit – LETOUR *hears what he's been waiting for:*
NEWSCASTER: (*Out of shot – radio*) This story is just in. A
    woman has fallen thirty stories to her death from a posh
    Grace Towers apartment on Lexington Avenue. Police are
    withholding identification pending the notification of the
    next of kin. The incident happened about ten p.m.
    According to the sources on the scene there was no one
    else in the posh Grace Towers apartment when the fall
    occurred. We will bring you more details as we get them.
    (*Teletype efx.*) An end to the sanitation strike seems
    imminent. Negotiations at the Helmsley Palace are
    continuing to this hour . . .
    (*Actions have consequences.*)

CUT TO:

MOTHER TERESA

First light. Jones Street. LETOUR, *sleepless, pounds on Teresa's*
door. No answer. Knocks again. Again.
Noises from inside. A sleepy voice:
TERESA: (*Out of shot*) Who is it?
LETOUR: John. John LeTour. Can I see you?
TERESA: (*Out of shot*) What time is it?
LETOUR: It's important, Teresa.
TERESA: (*Out of shot*) Call. Make an appointment.
LETOUR: Open the door. You're awake anyway.
    (*No answer.*)
    Teresa.
    (TERESA, *wearing oriental bathrobe, unlatches the door.* JOHN
    enters, turns to her. The door closes.)
LETOUR: Read me. What do you see?
TERESA: Do I know you?
LETOUR: We had a session last week. What do you see?
TERESA: (*Remembering name*) John?
LETOUR: Yes. Look at me.
    (TERESA *takes a moment to concentrate.*)
TERESA: Step back.
    (*He does.*)
    Again.

(*He does.*)
Death.

LETOUR: Someone I knew died tonight.

TERESA: This was not an accident. This person was murdered.

LETOUR: Am I in danger?

TERESA: (*Beat*) There is danger around you. It's very close. I'm
sleepy.

LETOUR: What should I do?

TERESA: I can't see it.

LETOUR: Please.
(*She shrugs.*)
Am I lucky?

TERESA: Yes. Don't be afraid. Go home.
(TERESA *shuffles toward her bedroom—the "reading" is over.*)

LETOUR: What do I owe you?

TERESA: Nothing. Forget it. Let me sleep.

CUT TO:

SNITCH

Mid-morning. LETOUR, *still awake, walks past towering Chelsea
trash.*
He passes a newsstand. Tabloids feature yearbook photo of
MARIANNE; *the headline: "Fall from Grace."*
LETOUR *walks to a pay phone, takes out Guidone's card, inserts a
quarter, dials.*

POLICE SWITCHBOARD: (*Out of shot*) Ninth Precinct.

LETOUR: Bill Guidone, please. Homicide.

POLICE SWITCHBOARD: (*Out of shot*) Hold on.
(JOHN, *suspicious, looks around.* GUIDONE *speaks:*)

GUIDONE: (*Out of shot*) Guidone.

LETOUR: This is John LeTour. Remember me?

GUIDONE: (*Out of shot*) Laundromat. Your father's got
connections.

LETOUR: You said I should ask around, tell you something you
didn't know.

GUIDONE: (*Out of shot*) I thought you'd call.

LETOUR: It ain't much, but it's something.

GUIDONE: (*Out of shot*) Go on.

LETOUR: A girl died last night. Lexington Ave.

48

GUIDONE: (*Out of shot*) The jumper. Druggie.

LETOUR: The news said she was alone in the apartment when she went out—she wasn't. It's a cover-up. There was someone else.

GUIDONE: (*Out of shot*) Who?

LETOUR: Who lives in the apartment?

GUIDONE: (*Out of shot*) You there?

LETOUR: That's all I know. You asked me to tell you something. I told you something. (*Hangs up.*)

CUT TO:

A LITTLE SLEEP

Noon. LETOUR *enters a West Village apartment building.*
He presses an intercom button. Robert's voice answers:

ROBERT: (*Out of shot*) Who is it?

LETOUR: Jack. Let me in.
(*The door buzzes.*

ROBERT *opens the door to his overdecorated apartment.* JOHN *looks around.* TONY, *Robert's younger, unattractive lover, sips coffee at the table.*)

ROBERT: Where have you been? We were worried.

LETOUR: I need some sleep—not much. I don't want to go home just yet. A little sleep first. Can I crash here? Nice place.

ROBERT: It's hideous. I did it years ago. I've got to throw everything out. You haven't been here?
(*Noticing* TONY.)
Oh, Jack, this is Tony. I told you about him. You should talk. He's the lapidopterist—gems.

TONY: (*Corrects him*) Lapidarian.

ROBERT: Same thing.

LETOUR: Can I?

ROBERT: Sure.

LETOUR: What do you know about Tis? What's his relationship to Ann?

ROBERT: They go way back—before me. Did you cross him?

LETOUR: No.

49

ROBERT: Don't. He's Ann's Ecstasy connection. She needs that score. What happened?

LETOUR: Nothing.

ROBERT: Don't mess with him.

LETOUR: Is he dangerous?

ROBERT: Everybody's dangerous. We heard what you did to Eddie. Ann thought it was great. She was afraid that was why you didn't come back.

LETOUR: It was something else. Tell me if you hear anything.

ROBERT: About what?

LETOUR: Tis.

ROBERT: Tis who? Ann says you want a chart done. (*Beat.*) What's wrong?

LETOUR: (*Internal*) Ah . . .

ROBERT: (*Sympathetic*) You down?

LETOUR: (*Nods*) Yeah . . . (*Culling thoughts.*) You ever think about it?

ROBERT: What?

LETOUR: That it'd be like this—like, your life, you . . . that it would turn out this way?—

ROBERT: Compared to what? My thinking this or that is going to make any difference? There's a plan unfolding. "Will my plane crash?" "Does life have meaning?"—why ask me? Thinking's a fear of living, negative living; living's something else. You're afraid. Let the plan unfold. Stop. Stop, live one day—one day—
(*Words blur to jargon.* LETOUR *cuts in:*)

LETOUR: —Robert—

ROBERT: —day at a time.

LETOUR: (*Touches* ROBERT) You've lost your fucking brain.

ROBERT: (*Laughs*) I'm a drug dealer.

LETOUR: Got a tub?

ROBERT: (*Gestures*) Yeah.

LETOUR: Great. (*Turns to bathroom.*)

ROBERT: There's a plastic bottle of bath oil in the cabinet. Yellow. Use it—tell me what you think. It's a new formula.

JUMP-OFFS

Six p.m. LETOUR, *shaved and bathed, rides a cab uptown, past Harlem, past 158th Street. He motions to the* DRIVER; *the taxi stops at a blue door between retail stores begging for renovation.* TEENAGE LATINOS *hang out.* LETOUR *gives the* CABBIE *a twenty.* LETOUR *walks to the blue door; the* YOUTHS *stop, watch. He knocks on the door. A* PUERTO RICAN DOORMAN *in white leather pants and a heart-shaped diamond ring opens the door, looks him over.* JOHN *reaches into his pouch, removes a gram envelope, hands it to him. The* DOORMAN *takes a taste, buzzes him through a door hand-lettered "Jump-Offs."*

Inside Jump-Offs, a cocaine "spot," every eye turns to JOHN: *the only Anglo in a Hispanic after-hours club. Tough young faces, each with a style and two inches of attitude. Willie Colon plays on the jukebox.*

Searching, LETOUR *recognizes a face, walks over:*

LETOUR: Manny.

> (MANUEL, *thirtyish, Puerto Rican, looks closer, trying to place* LETOUR.)

LeTour. (*Helping out.*) Jealous. "Jell." SOB's.

MANUEL: (*Remembering*) Reggae night.

LETOUR: Burning Spear.

MANUEL: How'd you get in?

LETOUR: C-C.

MANUEL: You buying?

LETOUR: How's product?

MANUEL: (*Gesture: "primo"*) How much?

LETOUR: I got a problem. I need a piece.

MANUEL: Piece? Piece of what? Piece of candy?

LETOUR: A gun.

MANUEL: When?

LETOUR: Now. Anything.

> (MANUEL *is silent.*)

Am I speaking too fast?

MANUEL: How much you spend?

LETOUR: The rate. What you got?

> (MANUEL *calls over a* TEENAGE DOMINICAN, *explains the*

situation in Spanish. The DOMINICAN *replies;* MANUEL *turns back to* JOHN:)

MANUEL: He's got a 64 Smith-son. Detective Special. Nobody wants 'em. Fresh from a cop.

LETOUR: How much?

MANUEL: (*Consults* DOMINICAN) Four—including me.

LETOUR: You're fucking me.

MANUEL: ("*So what?*") Street price.

LETOUR: Where is it?

MANUEL: Sigame.

(*They lead him to an even darker back room.*
The DOMINICAN *retrieves an automatic pistol from a trash pail, hands it to* MANUEL. JOHN *counts cash from Tis' roll;* MANNY *hefts the piece.*)

MANUEL: The hundreds—Franklins.

(*Bills and guns exchanged.*)

LETOUR: How do you use this?

MANUEL: Automatic.

LETOUR: I don't have much use for a gun. Never used one like this.

MANUEL: (*Translates for* DOMINICAN) Cono!

(*The* DOMINICAN *laughs;* LETOUR *takes his measure.*)

LETOUR: (*Businesslike*) What do you do?

MANUEL: Simple. You put the bullets in — (*Inserts cartridge.*) you point it at the bad guys, pull the trigger and they fall down!

(MANNY *repeats this for the* DOMINICAN *["bang, bang!"]; they laugh again.* LETOUR *eases the .38 into his crotch.*

MANNY *turns, exchanges Latin hug:*)

MANUEL: Vaya con Dios.

LETOUR: — Dios.

(JOHN *exits, works his way through the club.*)

CUT TO:

OUT WITH THE OLD

John's apartment. Seven p.m. LETOUR, *sweating, bareback, tucks the .38 under his futon.*

He takes a bottle of cologne from the bathroom, pours it over his hair, face, and torso, rubs it in.

Licking his finger, he removes Marianne's gold and onyx ring with a tug. His finger stings. He opens a window, throws the ring full force into the junk-strewn courtyard. He shakes his torso; cologne glistens.

CUT TO:

JOHN AND RANDI

Interior, Plaza Memorial Chapel. LETOUR *enters the "viewing room," motions to* RANDI. *She follows him.*

They slip into a door, enter the embalming room: stainless steel table surrounded by surgical cabinets.

They embrace, disengage. JOHN *looks: Randi's exhausted face mirrors his.*

LETOUR: Have you been to the police station?

RANDI: (*Nods*) She was back on drugs. Really back. They're gonna bring her here too. My God.

53

(*He comforts her.*)
I thought she was playing for attention.

LETOUR: I didn't know.

RANDI: You're not to blame. Don't blame yourself. You
weren't responsible. She was always—she loved you.

LETOUR: (*Wipes tear from her cheek*) She loved you. You were
what she wanted to be.

RANDI: She scared me.

(JOHN *pulls a Polaroid from his pocket.*)

LETOUR: Look. Do you recognize anyone?

(*The picture features* ANN *and* TIS: *side by side at a dinner party.*)

RANDI: Tis.

LETOUR: You know him?

RANDI: His father's a lawyer. Did some tax things for Mom. He was at the hospital. What's that smell?

LETOUR: It's me. Cologne. I'm a sucker for that cheap airplane stuff. Did Marianne mention him yesterday?

RANDI: (*"No"*) It was his apartment. What are you thinking?

LETOUR: I don't know.

RANDI: She jumped. (LETOUR *hangs on every word.*) You loved her, but she—this sounds terrible but it's true—she was . . . she ruined everything . . . bad luck.

LETOUR: (*Heard enough*) When's the funeral—your mother's?

RANDI: Tomorrow. Will you come?

LETOUR: (*Vague*) Well, I got this thing to do. It's—I don't know if I can get away.

RANDI: Try? For me.

LETOUR: I'll try.

CUT TO:

PRODIGAL SON

Ann's apartment. Eight p.m. ANN *greets* LETOUR *with a hug.*

ANN: The Prodigal Son.

LETOUR: Sorry about last night. Something came up.

ANN: Where were you?

LETOUR: T.C.T.E.

ROBERT: "Too Complicated To Explain."

LETOUR: (*Enters bedroom*) I'm $500 short from last night. I'll get it, you can take it from my salary.

ANN: (*Stung*) This is family. Are you saying that to hurt me?

(LETOUR *returns.*)

It's not money.

LETOUR: (*Chagrined*) Sorry.

ROBERT: Look at this. (*"Akasha" visual.*) We had a graphic artist make it up—you know, Billy, Five Towns.

55

ANN: The label for the cosmetics line.

LETOUR: (*Examines it*) Classy. Sorta—Katmandu . . .

ANN: (*Corrects him*) *Kath*mandu.

LETOUR: I love it.

ROBERT: Tis called twice. He wants you to come by.

LETOUR: (*Wary*) Me?

ANN: Yeah. Says you were supposed to show up again yesterday, but didn't.

LETOUR: A lie. I don't want to go. The suicide and all. Let's stay away.

ANN: Can't. He's the Ecstasy connect. No way I can fuck this.

LETOUR: C'mon . . .

ANN: This is business.

> (LETOUR, *suspicious, looks from* ANN *to* ROBERT. *He knows* TIS *knows he knows* MARIANNE *was not alone when she went out the window.*)

LETOUR: Let Robert go.

ANN: Tis won't deal with fags.

LETOUR: Since when?

ANN: Just is—so he's a bigot? What's new? So's everybody else.

LETOUR: I don't want to go. I got a bad vibe.

ROBERT: He said you.

ANN: (*To* LETOUR) Why?

LETOUR: (*To* ANN) Why don't you go? He's *your* contact.

ROBERT: He is—

ANN: (*To* ROBERT) You giving orders?

ROBERT: (*Deferential*) No, Missy.

LETOUR: (*Testing her*) Come with me—the two of us.

ANN: (*Upbeat*) Okay. You got it. Like old times—Ann and Johnny. (*Turns to go.*)

LETOUR: Okay.

ROBERT: Stop it. You're breaking my heart.

CUT TO:

LAST RIDE

Night. ANN *and* LETOUR *side by side in the sedan.* CARLOS, *at the wheel, anonymous. Outside,* SANITATION WORKERS *toss sacks of trash into garbage trucks: the strike is over.*

ANN *reminisces as lights flash:*

ANN: It's going to be strange, not doing this. I mean I've had it, but sometimes . . .

LETOUR: You're gonna do it, aren't you? You're gonna quit.

ANN: (*Nods*) I think so. Seal this thing with Tis, turn it–go with the cosmetics. You gotta take a chance in life. No risk, no gain. I've already got retail connections here, London. It was great at the beginning, though.

LETOUR: When?

ANN: You know, when we first started out of the place on Greene Street. Before deliveries, when you were still using. It was open house every night but Sunday. We had everything: uppers, downers, meth, six kinds of hash, all in that trousseau, remember? You could get in for a gram, stay all night–everybody, music people, movies, Wall Street, fashion–even politics. I think like five marriages came out of those parties, babies–really. God.
(JOHN *eyes her: why this Niagara, this nostalgia?*)
You stayed, you then Robert–but he . . . I'da never thought you'd, what is it, twelve years? Others, lucky a year max, eight months, in, out, start using, unreliable– nice kids. Remember when you first came: long hair, dirty fingers–

LETOUR: (*Overlapping*) You made me–

ANN: –never washed–

LETOUR: –khaki pants.

ANN: I should write a book someday. Did you know somebody wanted to do my story? Ghostwrite. It was impossible, of course–my lawyer freaked I even had the meeting. People envy me. They think my life is so glamorous, but they don't know. I know. *Glamorous.* (*Beat.*) It was for a while. Then came crack and fucked everything.
(JOHN *wonders: the Big Goodbye? Is she acting at Tis'
behest?*)

LETOUR: I gotta stop home a second.

ANN: Why? It's out of the way. They're expecting you.
(*"They're?"*)

LETOUR: You know I got a bad vibe about Tis.

ANN: (*Unconvincing*) Chill. This is routine.

57

LETOUR: I want to get my lucky jacket.

ANN: Oh. Okay.

(*The sedan continues south. It turns, stops in front of John's Chelsea apartment building.*

JOHN *hops out, goes in.*

Inside John's apartment he—a man possessed—pulls his black tweed from the closet, throws it on the futon. He rolls up his shirt, reaches under the futon, removes the .38.

He straps the gun to his back, wraps duct tape around his chest, end to end over the .38. He tucks in his shirt, puts on the jacket, checks the mirror to see if the gun shows: it doesn't. A pause to appreciate.

LETOUR *closes his diary, throws it out the window: a trifle. He slaps cologne on his cheeks—annointing; heads toward the door.*

Outside, LETOUR *emerges, walks quickly to the car, plops beside* ANN. *The sedan drives off. Back seat:*)

ANN: That took long enough. What did you do, douche while you were at it?

LETOUR: Ann, you got some mouth on you.

ANN: You don't want to know where it's been. (*Sniffs him.*) Cologne?

LETOUR: For you.

ANN: Phew. It smells like that stuff they give you on airplanes. It's no good for your skin. All chemicals.

(LETOUR *pulls out a slip of paper, writes a name and address: "Linda Wichel, 1012B-2 A Street, Sacramento, California."*)

ANN: What's that?

LETOUR: Do me a favor.

ANN: What?

LETOUR: Don't ask why, just promise.

ANN: What is it?

LETOUR: (*Testing again*) If anything happens to me—if I should like, you know, fucking die—write and tell her. (*Extends slip of paper.*

ANN *starts to speak, stops.*)

LETOUR: It's my sister. Her husband's in San Quentin. She worries, you know.

(*She takes the name and address.*)

ANN: (*Eye contact*) Okay.

(ANN, *sad, looks out the window. She touches his knee.*
The car pulls in front of the Pennsylvania Hotel, 34th and
7th.)

LETOUR: I thought we were going to Tis'?

ANN: We are. He's here. He can't very well work out of his
apartment after what happened yesterday, can he?

(*They get out.*)

CUT TO:

SHOOT-OUT

Pennsylvania lobby: a baseball card convention is in progress.
ANN *squeezes through, goes to the house phone.* JOHN *follows,*
scans the tacky lobby: what's up?

ANN: (*On phone*) Mathis Bruge, please. (*Beat.*) Tis? Ann. I'm
here with Tour. (*Beat.*) Okay. (*Hangs up.*)

LETOUR: Tis there?

ANN: Twelve-oh-four.

(*They go to the elevators, wait with* CHATTY CARD
COLLECTORS *[Pete Rose this, Pete Rose that].*
Twelfth floor. ANN *and* JOHN *step out of the elevator, look*
for 1204.
LETOUR, *a step behind, is all eyes, all ears.*
ANN *checks the number, rings the bell.*
THOMAS *lets them in the standard issue suite, locks the door.*
LETOUR *was right: it's a set-up.* THOMAS *and a* TEENAGE
CUBAN *stand either side of them, waistbands conspicuously*
bulging. No TIS. JOHN *turns to* ANN:)

LETOUR: (*Jesus-to-Judas*) Ann.

(ANN's *confused, then furious: she had no part in the "set-*
up." In fact, she doesn't even know it's a set-up.
Bursting rage, she turns on THOMAS, YELLS:)

ANN: I told you greasy fucks I don't deal with guns! I see
guns, I walk! How dare you?

(*She slaps* THOMAS, *pulls the 9mm from his waistband,*
throws it to the carpet.

59

The CUBAN *watches bewildered, gun drawn, awaiting instructions. Now* ANN's *on him:*)

ANN: And you, beaner, whoever the fuck you are, kiss my fat ass!

(She spits on his shirt, knees him in the crotch, yanks his gun, throws it beside the gut-clutching CUBAN. *She crosses the room, YELLING:*)

That's it! TIS! Shitball! I know you're fucking there! Let this be a lesson! You wanna deal, you gonna apologize for this!

(To LETOUR.)

Let's go.

(THOMAS *and the* CUBAN TEEN *retrieve their guns;* ANN *unlocks the door.*)

THOMAS: *(Pointing gun)* Hold it! Stop right there.

(She turns defiantly. TIS *enters from bedroom:*)

TIS: *(To* THOMAS) No!

(To ANN.)

Sorry about the guns. My fuck-up. I was just trying to make a point — I apologize.

(TIS *looks to* THOMAS *and the* CUBAN: *they lower their weapons. He only means to threaten* LETOUR.)

60

TIS: (*About* THOMAS *and* CUBAN) Assholes. What a nightmare.
(*To* ANN.)
We'll make the deal tomorrow—same terms. Ann. Sorry.
Go on, leave, you're upset. I just need to talk to Tour a
second. About a police matter.
(*To* LETOUR.)
Right?

LETOUR: (*To* ANN) Go on.
(*She hesitates.*)

TIS: Tour and I need to get our stories straight. Somebody's
talking to the police. The guns were for emphasis, to
make a point, dumb—
(ANN *gets it. Fear hits:*)

ANN: (*To* TIS) *We* came together, *we're* leaving together.
(*To* LETOUR.)
Johnny, come with me. (*Opens door.*)

TIS: (*A command*) Thomas.
(THOMAS *fixes his gun on* ANN.)

TIS: (*To* ANN) Don't be stupid. Get out. Leave.
(*To* LETOUR.)
I had nothing to do with Marianne—she jumped: she was
there, then she was gone.
(*Nods* ANN *to leave.*)
Nothing will happen to Tour.
(ANN *computes, bolts out, flees, SCREAMING at the top of
her lungs:*)

ANN: (*Out of shot*) Fire! Fire! Fire!
(*The fire bell rings.*
THOMAS, TIS, *and the* CUBAN *stare dumbfounded.*
LETOUR *reaches behind his shirt in the confusion, yanks out
the .38 with a painful rip, turning, fires point-blank into the
Cuban's chest. BLAM! Shirt fabric flares, flies: the* CUBAN
falls with blank expression.
THOMAS, *off guard, wheels and* fires *wildly at* LETOUR.
JOHN *fires back. Both are hit.* TIS *ducks into the bedroom.*
THOMAS *and* LETOUR *fire again, again—hitting, missing.
A bullet hits its mark:* THOMAS, *frozen, grabs his blood-
spurting throat, slumps to floor.*
LETOUR *bleeds from the stomach and shoulder. His shirt*

soaks red; he struggles to stand. CUBAN *and* THOMAS — *both dead.* LETOUR *checks the .38: five rounds fired — one left.* LETOUR *staggers into the bedroom, finds* TIS *frantically searching an open suitcase. Off-screen* VOICES *under the fire bell.*)

TIS: (*Desperate*) I didn't —

(LETOUR *steps to* TIS, *aims, shoots him barrel to forehead. Exit debris hits the wall. He is dead.*

Off-screen screams of guests are countered by commands from hotel security: "Get down!" "Get back!" Fire horns and sirens reverb from the street.

LETOUR, *losing consciousness, sits bedside. Gun slips from his hand.*

Deflating, he drifts back-first to the bedspread. Blood spreads. His eyes are open.

POLICE VOICES *approach.*)

EVERY GRAIN OF SAND

Prison waiting area. ANN, *wearing a wool suit, waits among black/Hispanic* FRIENDS *and* RELATIVES. *The first scene without* LETOUR: *she sits quietly. A* CORRECTIONS OFFICER *instructs the visitors to proceed.*

ANN *walks through a concrete corridor, finds the visiting area.*
LETOUR, *in prison fatigues, sits at a table. He sees her, smiles.*
ANN *sits down. This is not her first visit.*
LETOUR: Hello.
ANN: Hi. (*Checks watch.*)
LETOUR: Twenty minutes. You look terrific.
ANN: I look respectable. Any news?
LETOUR: Sentencing's in ten days—supposed to be. Because of the extenuating circumstances—our cooperation—they say it won't be more than five years—maybe seven. With time served, good behavior, parole, I could be out in two years—maybe. I hope.
ANN: It feels like forever.
LETOUR: It's not so bad. It's a relief in a way—at least so far. I've been writing, reading.
ANN: I love your letters. (*Pause.*)
LETOUR: How's business?
ANN: Robert quit. He went back to dealing. I think he thought it would be less work, more money. It's lucky in a way I got mixed up in it—now I have to see this thing through. So it's cosmetics after all.
LETOUR: (*Affectionate*) I miss you.
ANN: Me too.
LETOUR: Did we ever fuck?
ANN: What do you mean?
LETOUR: You know, make love.
ANN: (*Thinks*) There was that party when everybody was so stoned, but—oh yeah, that night you came over and crashed and we slept together.
LETOUR: We were naked, but did we—?
ANN: You had a hard-on . . .

63

LETOUR: I didn't—

ANN: You tried . . .

LETOUR: I was thinking about it and I realized we never really did. It's one of the things I think about. It's one of the things I look forward to. I've been looking forward.

ANN: Me too.

LETOUR: (*Touches her hand*) Something can be right in front of you and you can't see it.

ANN: (*Kisses his hand*) Strange how things work.

(*The tableau fades.*)